TOCABAGA 10

POWER OF THE SWORD

Potestas Gladii

THOMAS H. WARD

TOCABAGA 10:

POWER OF THE SWORD

by

THOMAS H. WARD

ISBN-13: 978-0692436363

ISBN-10: 0692436367

Transcendent Publishing
www.transcendentpublishing.com

PREFACE

As stated in my earlier chronicles the United States is in a state of chaos, and extreme turmoil. We came to this because of an overzealous President and a Congress that sat by and did nothing to protect our rights.

The President put into effect Presidential Executive Order 13603, which to everyone's surprise declares that all property belongs to the Federal government, your house, money, guns, and even your kids. They can tell you where to live and where to work.

Back in 2013 the NSA started to tap our phones, reading our emails, reading our snail mail, reading our face book page. We were all being watched, we were all suspected of doing something wrong, we were all having our Bill of Rights violated in the name of government security, and no one did anything about it.

Benjamin Franklin once said, "He who sacrifices freedom for security deserves neither."

Thank God, the US Military believes Executive Order 13603 violates the US Constitution. The Army Rangers are fighting with us to gain control back from the Federal Police, al-Qaida, and numerous gangs. We will win this fight, we will never surrender, and we will persevere.

I love our country, freedom, my family, and friends. If anyone messes with my family, or friends, justice will be swift and painful. I have no use for anyone who breaks the law, cheats or steals. For the most part I follow the Ten Commandments, but also believe in The Code of Hammurabi, which is an eye for an eye. I fight to keep our Bill of Rights under the United States Constitution. That is me, Jack Gunn, a.k.a. Tocabaga Jack, and these are my chronicles.

I am Director of Security for Tocabaga Island. I live here along with 556 other Patriots, we are fighting to keep our freedom, keep our homes, and keep our families safe from the evil forces gone wild. Tocabaga is a sanctuary or safe haven. If you believe in the Constitution, the Bill of Rights, and are of good moral character you are welcome here.

We are waiting for you to contact us by email to find out where Tocabaga is located. Sending us an email is your first step to Freedom. There is an email address in these chronicles. Tocabaga is a real location. I will reply.

Jack Gunn

COMMENTARY

The world is made up of invisible forces, all of which have a positive and negative side. They can be good or bad forces. You say, invisible forces, what a bunch of bull crap.

I can name a few. To start with, consider the wind. You can't see it, you cannot taste it, but you can feel the air or wind blowing ever so invisible. The wind of a hurricane or tornado can destroy whole cities. It's a very powerful force. The wind in a Tornado can be seen in directly by the dirt swirling around. The wind blowing can be felt or seen by looking at the trees. The wind can also be a good force bringing needed rain or coolness to the desert. The opposite of the wind is no wind, which also can be a positive or negative force of nature.

Next consider magnetism. A magnetic field is invisible to your eye yet the earth's magnetic field can affect anything that is magnetic, like a compass. A magnetic field has a North and South Pole. There is an invisible magnetic field covering the earth protecting it from the solar winds and radiation from the sun. This field is caused by the molten iron core in the center of the earth. Most people give no thought to this powerful invisible force here on earth. In a magnetic field there is an attraction, or positive end, and a repulsion, or negative end.

Another great invisible force is electricity. If you touch it and get shocked, you know it's there, but you can't normally see this great invisible force. If it arcs or shorts then it may spark. Like the other invisible forces, electricity has positive and negative sides which can repel each other.

Gravity is the invisible force of attraction that one physical object has over another because of its mass. Everyone and everything on earth is under the influence of gravity. Objects in space are in orbit due to gravity. What goes up must come down.

It is a scientific theory that Dark Matter is a type of matter that makes up 84% of the Universe. It does not absorb light or emit light so it cannot be seen by the human eye. What if there are other so called dark matter objects, things, people, or beings? Is this possible?

The world and the universe could be made up of many other types of invisible forces that we don't know about because we can't see them. It might be possible there are beings, or life forms, we cannot see with our eyes living among us here on earth. Some may call them angles, spirits, or ghosts.

Every now and then, when conditions are right, we can obtain a split second glimpse of them.

Invisibles could be all over the earth. I think they can see us, but we can't see them. They might follow certain people and watch over them for some reason.

Are they God's Angles? I don't know, but I do know there are supernatural forces at work here on earth.

THOMAS H. WARD

SUMMARY

I haven't made an entry in over a month. I've been busy working with Adam de Molay, my adopted grandson, trying to influence his strange thinking and grandiose plans. He needs to be kept busy at all the time. Adam has a type 'A' personally, like me, but he's mentally disturbed from years of physical and mental abuse from his father.

Adam's grandfather, was the Grand Master of the Knights Templar, until he passed away a short time ago. Everyone thought the Templars no longer existed. Adam's blood line dates back to the last Templar Grand Master who was Jacques de Molay. He was burned at the stake in 1314.

Everyone on Tocabaga has been busy getting ready for the Arctic Vortex to arrive. The temperature has dropped a little below normal and is definitely cooler at night. The cold weather seems to be slowly inching south. The question is: will it keep coming or stop? Perhaps SOCOM can provide some insight on the future of the weather.

We've seen more hordes of people moving south, driving or walking, down the expressway. Every now and then a group shows up at our

Tocagaba Bridge. We provide them some food and supplies that we can spare. Some groups demand entrance, which causes a conflict. Most of the hordes appreciate our help and move on in a few days.

The guard dogs we found are working out well. My dog, Adolf, was a blessing for the whole family. Being a light sleeper every little noise would wake me up. With big Adolf guarding the door, I didn't worry about anything unless he lets out a bark.

I haven't slept this well in years.

RECAP OF MY LAST ENTRY
ON AUGUST 4, 2025

While on a hunting trip, we encountered Jack de Molay the Grand Master of the Knights Templar. He was an old sick old man who died after a few hours after meeting us. Before he died, Jack de Molay told me it was God's wish that I take care of his grandkids after he passed. Somehow he knew my name, even though I had never meant him before.

Adam is twelve years old and is large for his age. He's a good looking kid with blond hair and bright blue eyes. He's smart as a whip and is a quick learner. His sister, Emma, is a cute little eight year old girl with long curly light-brown hair.

I brought Jack's grandkids, Adam and Emma, back to live with my family on Tocabaga. We soon found out that Adam de Molay had serious mental issues and illusions of grandeur. I decided to try and bond with him to see if he presented any dangers for the citizens of Tocabaga.

I took Adam to see the Tocabaga church since he expressed an interest in it. Adam and I sat in the church speechless for a few minutes as he looked around. I decided to press the issue about the Templar Knights. "Adam, tell me about the Knights Templar."

Adam looked at me and didn't answer right away. I guess he was thinking what to tell me. "The Templar Order is a secret society. We are on a mission for God. The Knights Templar main mission is to restore the United States of America to be one nation under God. We're a country founded on Christian-Judeo beliefs. We will help restore our country to its greatness."

"I like what you said ... but how will you do that?" Now I was really concerned about what he was planning. He's just a kid and thinking this way could be dangerous.

Adam gave a sigh, like it was all too boring for him to explain. "Ok, I'll tell you the theory or premise since you're my guardian. The reason the country fell apart is because we lost our way. We lost our direction and didn't follow God's teachings or commandments. The country became evil.

"We removed prayers from schools and removed the word God or Christ from our books. We didn't teach anything about Christ or God. We took down the Ten Commandments from courtrooms and schools. We took the Christ out of Christmas and made it just another holiday."

"Yes, I agree with that," I replied.

"The Templar Knights are God's Warriors. We must destroy any person who does not believe in God. There must be a purging of the evil ones from the United States."

I thought, H*oly shit! This kid is nuts.* "How are you going to purge the evil ones?"

Adam was now walking around in circles, as if he was worked up into a frenzy.

He continued, "The Templar Army is now spreading out across the United States. The Order I was with will be based in Florida, just south of here, in Bradenton. That's where Hernando de Soto landed in 1539. De Soto was a Templar Knight. In due time, I'll start another Order enlisting at least a thousand men."

This kid has been brainwashed by his Father into thinking he would be the savior of the United States. I felt sorry for him because I knew his brain was consumed with the idea he was God's Warrior. Adam could prove to be a very dangerous person to have on Tocabaga.

Adam continued by asking, "Do you believe in reincarnation?"

"By reincarnation, do you mean coming

back to life in a different body?"

"Yes, that's what I mean."

"Well, I don't know. I've never died, as far as I know." I gave a little chuckle, thinking what I said was funny.

Adam looked at me with a stern face. "Jesus was born again. He came back reincarnated after three days in a different body. No one but his close friends knew who he was. Then he ascended to heaven. I'm living proof of reincarnation. I was reincarnated from the Jacques de Molay blood line, as was my father and grandfather."

"Adam, exactly how do you know that?"

"I know that because secrets and ancient relics have been passed down over the generations. We have the Templars' Treasure."

"If you have the Templars' Treasure taken from Jerusalem, tell me about it."

"I can't tell you; it's a secret. Only a few people know what it is. I can tell you the treasure items prove that God is real. It verifies the Old and New Testament."

"Ok, I believe in God. You don't need to convince me. What I don't agree with is what you wanna do. You want to destroy anyone who doesn't believe in God. That's not what the United States is about. We have freedom of religious expression to believe in God or not. The country was founded by pilgrims fleeing religious persecution."

I hoped what I said would sink into his brain. His thinking was way out there.

Adam responded, "Yes, I know all that, but we need to go to extremes to bring us back to normal. What about people like radical Islamists? There's al-Qaida and ISIS who would gladly cut off your head if you don't convert to their form of Islam."

"We've done battle with al-Qaida. I agree they need to be eliminated. Perhaps, you should lead your Templars in that direction. To me, that makes a lot more sense."

Adam stopped pacing and sat down. He seemed to be contemplating what I had just told him. "What you say is true. They will be our first target," Adam said.

I replied, "They should be your only target. You can't go around killing people because they don't believe in God. You'll make a lot of enemies, including the United States Army and the people living here on Tocabaga."

Adam replied, "You've given me a lot to think about. I'll pray and see what God tells me."

"Ok, you pray on it. It's getting late, so let's go home."

On the way home Adam said, "Thank you for the talk. You remind me of my Grandpa."

I didn't say a word as I put my arm around his shoulder and we slowly walked home.

I never thought this kid would be a big nut case, but he's messed up. On the other hand, it would be nice to have a counterforce to fight the never ending attacks of the radical forces of ISIS and al-Qaida. There are thousands of them slowly taking over parts of the country to create their own Islamic State. The Knights Templar could help quell the extremists.

We arrived home and ate dinner. I usually say the prayer at dinner, but I let Adam say grace. After eating I rounded up my male family members and we went to the Green Room. I had to tell them what Adam had revealed to me. I needed to seek some advice.

I informed them of Adam's thinking and everyone was pretty much surprised. Ron commented that the kid freaked him out. Tommy told us Adam would probably outgrow the ideas that were drummed into his head by his grandfather.

I told them that I didn't think he'd outgrow his crazy ideas. They were beaten into him. He's been mentally damaged. I suggested we have to keep Adam busy all the time so he can't dwell on being a Templar Knight. We need to teach him fishing, farming, hunting, and even start him on guard duty training. These activities, along with his schooling, might help him. I asked my family to tell their wives about Adam and to keep a close eye on him.

I sat alone on the patio having a smoke while writing a work schedule for Adam. I'll keep him very busy like the other kids. The only difference is he'll be closely monitored.

God hasn't spoken to me yet. Until he does, I'll do what I think is best for Adam and Tocabaga.

Maybe, I'll pray a little more.

SEPTEMBER 10, 2025

I've been slowly bonding with Adam. He hasn't spoken again about the Templar Treasure. Adam was going to pray and ask God for direction, ever since I told him he couldn't terminate all nonbelievers. So far he hasn't mentioned if God has spoken to him.

Adam has been very busy with school, working on the farm, learning how to fish, and pulling kitchen duty. He seems to be getting along well with the other children. Johnny started to teach him how to play baseball. Adam is coming around, but it's going to take some time.

While working in the kitchen he met Rahim, the only Muslim man living on Tocabaga. Months ago Rahim moved here with his family for protection after almost being killed by al-Qaida. Rahim is a gentle giant who believes in non-violence. They seem to be getting along fine. Maybe working with Rahim will change his thinking about Muslims. Adam may come to realize most are peaceful honest people.

Adam needs to keep his strong faith in God, but also needs to believe in the idiom, 'live and let live.' Keeping that in mind, he shouldn't forget 'an eye for an eye.' If someone does you wrong, then justice needs to be served.

It was 2 pm and I was on guard duty at the bridge. We observed an old pick-up truck coming down the road. It pulled up to the fence and stopped. Two men jumped out and yelled my name, "Jack Gunn! Is Jack Gunn here?"

Adolf was sitting at my side. He could sense these people were strangers and let out a growl. I tightly held his leash as he stood up and tugged at it.

I carefully observed the strangers. They didn't have rifles, but carried side-arms. Four of my guards at the fence turned and looked back at me, waiting for my response. Picking up my M4, I slowly walked down to the fence to see what these guys wanted.

My mind was racing because they knew my name and I didn't know who they were. Approaching the ten-foot high chain link fence, I noticed these men seemed nervous. They kept scanning around the area and then would look back at their truck.

Standing a few feet away from them, looking through the chain links, they appeared to be your standard Free Roamers. Free Roamers who would kill you for a nickel. Both men had a dirty unkempt appearance.

They had on dirty jeans and T-shirts that had holes because they were so old. One had on a cap that had a Seal Trident on it. The other man had on a black leather jacket and a boonie hat with long brown hair hanging down. They were weathered tough looking dudes. Both wore wrap-around sun glasses.

I said, "I'm Jack Gunn. What's up?"

The one with the Seal hat replied, "Someone told us you were in charge here. We got something for you."

Gazing at their faces, I pulled out a pack of smokes, lit up a butt, and took a drag while trying to seem unconcerned. "Who told you my name?"

The guy in the Seal cap replied, "It doesn't matter who told me."

"What do you have?" I took a deep drag and blew the smoke in their direction.

"I'll tell you, but first I need your agreement to help us out."

"Tell me what you want. Then I decide if I'll

help you."

"We want guns for what we're gonna give you."

"Step closer to the fence and take off those sun glasses," I told them. They moved up to the fence and removed their glasses. "Chris, take their temperature." Chris pulled out his thermo scanner and aimed it at each man.

"Hey, what's that?" Boonie hat man asked.

"It's a thermometer. We're checking you for Ebola," Chris said. "They check out OK, Jack."

Unlocking the gate, I went out with Adolf by my side. My men followed me to meet these guys face to face. Stepping up to the man with the Seal cap on, I coldly peered into his bloodshot eyes. "Ok, dork. Tell me what you have and I'll decide whether to help you or not."

The guy said, "My name is Reed Gurra." He stuck out his hand for me to shake with a little smirk on his face.

Adolf let out a growl. Glancing at his hand I noticed a Seal ring on his finger. I could tell they were junkies by their red eyes. I didn't stick my hand out, ignoring his offer to shake. After a second he withdrew it. This guy was no Navy Seal and I wondered how he came by the ring.

Reed said, "Do we have your word that you'll help us out?"

"You have my word." I didn't mind lying to a dirt bag wearing a Seal ring that he didn't earn. "Where'd you get that ring and hat from?"

"I was a Navy Seal," Reed replied.

"Mister, you're no Navy Seal. You're a fucking liar."

"Nobody calls me a liar." Reed slowly moved his hand towards his pistol.

Adolf lunged at him bearing his teeth while barking. I held him back as I flicked off my safety and pointed the M4 at Reed's belly. "You draw that gun and you're dead, shithead." My men immediately raised their weapons pointing them at both jerks.

Raising his hands a little Reed replied, "Ok, you're right. So what, I'm not a Seal." He had that smirk on his face again.

"Both of you, keep your hands up." I motioned to Chris. "Take their guns." Chris frisked them both and collected their weapons. Each had two cheap handguns that weren't worth a shit, and a knife.

Reaching down, I grabbed Reed's hand. "Give me that ring or I'll cut off your finger." Of course he gave it to me. I snatched the Seal cap off his head.

"Ok, asshole, what do you want?"

"We know where your buddy Rico is," Reed said.

"You better talk fast, Mister. Where is he?"

Reed pointed at my M4. "First, give us fifty of those guns, along with some ammo. Then I'll tell you where you can find him."

I stepped up to him and in one swift movement whacked him in the throat with the side of my hand. Reed fell to his knees gasping for breath while holding his neck. "Tell me where Rico is or you're gonna feel a lot more pain."

Gasping for air he said, "Hey ... a deal ... is a ... deal."

I kicked him hard as I could in the face. "I don't honor deals with dirt bags." Reed was knocked out.

Stepping over to the other shithead I asked,

"What's your name boy?"

He looked at his friend lying on the ground with blood running from his broken nose. "Freddy Hammon."

"Freddy, where's Rico?"

He looked down again at his buddy. "I can't tell you. He'll kill me if I do."

"Freddy, don't worry about him killing you. I'm gonna kill you right now if you don't talk."

Pulling out my double edged Black Bear, I waved the shiny Bowie blade in front of his face. Holding it up to his throat, I pressed it into his skin until he could feel the sharpness. Blood started to trickle down his neck.

"Freddy, have you ever seen a man bleed to death?" I could feel his whole body tremble. "It isn't a pretty sight to watch. I want you to have a lot of pain."

Freddy said, "Look … in the truck. There's a message and a knife you need to see."

I decided to stop picking on him and removed the blade. "I hope you're not wasting my fucking time." I looked at Chris. "Check their truck. See what you can find."

Chris went to the truck and a few minutes later he brought me a Black Bear knife. I've only seen two Black Bears in my life, mine, and Rico's. It was Rico's alright, his name was on it.

Chris handed me a piece of paper. "Jack, you better read this note."

It read:

'If you kill my men your buddy is good as dead. You give us the guns and we give you Rico. If my men don't return by 6 pm kiss his ass good-bye. Come to the address below after six to find your buddy.'

The note was signed by Dirty Dan who was the 22nd Avenue gang leader. Dirty Dan had a reputation of being a cold blooded killer. He was a bully and ruled his gang by pure force. The two men here must be his trusted lieutenants.

I told Chris, "Tie them up."

As they were tying up Freddy he put up a little struggle. "Hey, what are you gonna do to us?"

I didn't reply.

Gazing at the note again, I couldn't believe the address that was on it. It was my father's old house. It's located deep in gang territory. The good thing, however, I knew that house like the back of my hand. My brother and son also knew the neighborhood. If Rico was there we could rescue him. I needed a plan.

Reed woke up. "If you kill us your buddy is dead." He had another smirk on his face. I wanted to hurt him real bad by smashing in his ugly face. I kicked Reed a couple of times in the face to shut him up.

Approaching Freddy I hit him hard in the gut. He doubled over gasping. I asked him, "Where are you taking the guns?"

Freddy hesitated for a minute. "To a safe house … on 23rd Avenue."

"How many men are guarding Rico?"

"I don't know for sure."

"Chris, blindfold them and take them inside the high and dry for a while."

By this time all my key men had arrived at the bridge watching what was going on. After passing around the note for everyone to read, I asked, "Anyone got any ideas how to save Rico without giving away our guns?"

Tommy said, "You know it could be a trap,

but I got an idea. For this operation I suggest we flank them. We'll have two Hummers come in from the south. I don't think they'll expect an attack from the south because the streets are almost impassable. The attack will be a distraction."

Mike asked, "A distraction from what?"

"While the Hummers attack the house, from the south side, Jack and two men will rescue Rico." Everyone gazed at Tommy like he was nuts.

"Go ahead," I said.

"The Hummers will leave now and move into position before 6 pm. We'll load up a gun box with rocks on the bottom and a layer of broken guns on top. We'll remove the bolts. They won't notice the difference."

"That sounds like a good idea," I said.

"Yeah, we'll let them see the guns in the box as they're loaded into their truck. When they leave, Jack and two men will leave right behind them, keeping out of sight.

"Jack, you take the F-250 we lined with armor plate."

The plan was hatched. As soon as my pickup rolled up to the house the Hummers would open fire with the fifty caliber guns creating confusion. We hoped the machine gun fire would draw whatever men were guarding Rico to the back yard. In the meant time, Mike and I would enter the front door, while Chris guarded our get-away vehicle.

It was the best plan we could muster in a short time. Time was running out so we had to hurry.

Glancing at my watch it was 4:30 pm. We needed to load up. The Hummers would leave 30 minutes before us to get into position. The dirt bags would leave at 5:30 pm.

Along with Adolf, I walked over to the high and dry. I told Reed and Freddy that we were going to supply the guns they wanted. Standing next to Freddy, I asked him, "What does Dirty Dan look like?"

"Don't tell him nothing, Freddy," Reed said, while spitting blood out of his mouth.

I yelled, "Shut the fuck up or I'll cut out your tongue! Well, Freddy, what's he look like?"

"Dan always wears a green Army beret. He has a gray beard and he's big."

"What do you mean big?"

"Dirty Dan is six foot three and weighs over 400 pounds. You can't miss him."

"Will he be at the house?"

"I don't know."

"Ok dorks, my men are getting the guns ready now. We'll let you leave at 5:30."

Grabbing both men by the front of the shirt, I pulled them up close to my face. I hissed, "If anything happens to Rico, I'll be coming after you and Dirty Dan. You can tell him that."

Our battle ready Hummers left for the house while I was talking to the dirtbags. Once our Humvees were out of sight, Chris dragged them back to their truck. It was almost 5:30 when my men brought out the box of guns.

While loading them into the truck, I swung open the lid. "Reed, go ahead, look inside."

Reed peeked in the box and said, "Looks, OK to me." I closed the lid and put a lock on it.

I put a lock on the box so Reed couldn't tamper with the goods and it would take them a little time to open it.

I cut their zip ties and said, "Get the hell out

of here."

Reed replied, "What about our pistols?"

"They're ours now. Leave before I change my mind."

Adolf snarled at them as the hair on his back rose up. He wanted a piece of these guys. Reed and Freddy quickly jumped in the old truck and drove away. After five minutes Chris, Mike, and I followed behind them at a safe distance. We saw them exit at 22nd Avenue and watched them turn south to 23rd Avenue.

Chris floored our F-250 as we went straight down 22nd Avenue. I got on the radio to Tommy when we were ten blocks away from the house. "Open fire we're ten blocks out." Approaching the house, I could hear our machine guns firing. We came to a screeching halt at the front door.

Mike and I jumped out while Chris took cover next to the vehicle, providing a rear guard. We ran to the front door which was wide open. I stuck my head inside and peeked around, but no one was there. Our fifty rounds were punching some holes in the backside of the house. I radioed, "Tommy, cease fire. We're going in." I was a little concerned that one of our rounds could hit Rico if he was there.

Scanning around the rooms, we didn't find a single person. I went to the back door and found Tommy standing there. "We didn't see anyone. Did you?" he asked.

"No, there's no one here," I said.

Tommy came inside and swung open the door to the secret room located behind the fireplace. I followed him in. "Well, there's no Rico. Damn it anyhow," he said. Much to our dismay the room was empty.

I took off my hat to wipe the sweat off my head and tried to think what the hell was going on. "Look around for any clues." Searching through the house we found a lot of old papers and junk. It was clear someone had been here. Then I saw it. There was a note tacked over the fire place. I read it out loud. 'Thanks for the guns. They helped your buddy.' It was signed by Dirty Dan. "What does he mean, they helped your buddy?"

Tom replied, "Maybe ... Rico's dead."

"Yeah, maybe, but let's leave before Mr. Dirty finds out he only got a few junk guns and some rocks."

Chris yelled, "Hey, some cars are coming."

We mounted up and made a fast escape

taking the winding back streets to 54th Avenue and then to Tocabaga. The Dirty Dan gang was hot on our heels.

We had no sooner pulled over the Tocabaga Bridge when Mike shouted, "They're still coming!"

Tommy and Mike turned the Hummer fifties on them and started to blast away. Dirty Dan's convoy came to a dead stop as fifty rounds slammed into their cars 400 yards away. They turned around and left, leaving one burning car in the street. I guess Mr. Dirty didn't wanna fight after all.

We went to the Green Room for a much needed night cap. I pulled the Seal ring out of my pocket and carefully looked at it. Engraved on the inside was a name. I slipped it on my finger. I'll wear Rico's ring until I find him.

I made my mind up, right then and there, that somehow I'll get Dirty Dan. Someday I'll find out what happened to Rico. Mr. Dirt Bag will pay dearly for this.

THOMAS H. WARD

SEPTEMBER 13, 2025

A few days have passed since our run in with the Dirty Dan gang. We've had many discussions about how to capture him and make him talk. I wanted to do something, but I didn't know exactly what. The rest of my warriors weren't so keen on risking another life to find out what happed to Rico. I can't say that I blame them. It's been a while since his disappearance.

If I was going to do anything, it would have to be on my own. I knew Tommy and Mike would come with me but it would be a dangerous mission. I had to think about this for a while.

It was a bright sunny day. So far the Arctic Vortex has had very little effect on our weather. It's a few degrees cooler but nothing serious.

I was sitting on my patio talking to my wife about Rico. She said, "I don't want you risking your life anymore to find out what happened to Rico. You have to face it, he's dead. You need to take care of your family; the hell with that eye for an eye bullshit."

"Your right honey. The problem is, I don't know if he's alive or not. It haunts me every day."

"Forget it, Jack. Don't you dare go searching for him. Every time you leave the island I don't know if you're coming back or not. I'm sick of it. You could be the next one to get killed."

As she stormed out of the room I replied, "You're right honey." There's no sense in arguing, since she's always right.

Sitting by myself, I was thinking about what Hemmi just told me. It must be hell for her every time I leave Tocabaga. I can see the worry lines on her face. It's starting to age her. As for myself, I never think about dying. If you do, then you're a dead man.

My radio came on, startling me. "Jack, you better come to the main bridge. I think we got trouble."

I grabbed my M4 and Adolf by the leash. Jumping in the truck I beat a path to the bridge. When I saw who was there I just about shit my pants.

Parked at the security fence were four Humvees, just like ours. In addition, there were five pick-up trucks loaded with armed men. They were dressed in black-colored special ops gear. These guys were no rag tag group of men. They all wore the same clothing with ballistic vests. They had an American flag patch on their shoulder. Glancing at their weapons, I saw M4s and a couple of M249 SAW's. These guys looked like pros' for sure.

My guards at the fence were talking to a guy holding a white flag with a red cross on it. I looked at the flag and knew immediately what it meant. With Adolf by my side, I walked down to the fence. Chris said, "Jack, this man wants to see you."

I said, "Chris, check him for Ebola."

"I already did. He's clean."

"Ok. Let him in." The big man walked through the gate leaving his guns and flag behind.

He approached me with a smile on his face. Standing three feet away, he bowed. "Greetings, Mr. Gunn. My name is Christian de Molay."

I thought, *is he related to Adam?*

Adolf at my side, didn't growl at the stranger. He just sat there watching his every move. Christian was a gigantic man standing about six and a half feet tall. He had a square face and long blond hair with a long beard. His blue eyes were small compared to the size of his head. His body was shaped and muscular in appearance. Hanging at his side was the tell tale broadsword.

The Broadsword was first manufactured in the 6th Century. It has a two-edged blade, measuring 2-3 inches wide at the base, with a tapered point. The length ranges from 30 - 45 inches. It weights between three to five pounds. The weapon is primarily used for cutting or slicing an opponent and is capable of cutting off the limbs or head of an enemy in one stroke.

I replied, "Please call me, Jack."

"You may call me Christian."

"How can I help you, Christian?"

"I had a hard time tracking you down, but I finally found you. I understand that you have Adam and Emma here."

"Yes, that's correct. You must be related to them."

"I'm their uncle. I'm on a mission to save them."

"I didn't know they had an uncle. Adam

never mentioned it."

"Well, I have never actually met Adam and Emma. Most likely my father never mentioned me, since I was an outcast. Now that my father has passed, I have accepted my heritage. I've taken over as the Templar Grand Master."

I thought, *what the hell?* "Wait a minute. You were an outcast. What's that mean?"

"Jack, it's a long story, but it's a family matter, that doesn't concern you."

"I'm sorry, but it does concern me since Adam is under my protection."

Christian laughed a little. "I'm their lawful uncle. They're under my protection."

I saw the sweat dripping down his face. I replied, "Let's sit over in the shade and discuss this."

I grabbed two bottles of water from a nearby cooler and handed him one. Sitting down in the shade of the bridge, I peered into his blue eyes to see if he was telling the truth. I twisted the cap off the bottle and said, "Enjoy."

He replied, "Thank you very much." We touched bottles together and took a deep swig.

"That's good. Could you provide my men some water?"

That comment was a good sign. It showed he cared about his men sitting out in the hot sun. It showed he was a sensitive person. "Sure. How many men do you have?"

"Twenty-four."

I called Chris over and asked him to give each man a bottle of water.

Christian commented, "Thank you for your kindness."

I asked, "Do you know how I met Adam and Emma?"

"No, not really. I was told that you took them when my father died. I feared that something terrible might happen to them."

"Well, this is a strange story, but true. My little group of hunters happened to come upon the Templars who were camped on the side of the road. An old man came up to me and asked for food. It was your father, Jack de Molay. He knew my name was Jack Gunn, but we had never met."

I took a swig of water and lit up a smoke. I offered one to Christian but he declined it. After taking a deep drag, I continued, "Jack believed that God sent me to protect Adam and Emma. It was strange because my dog Adolf was friendly to them and usually he doesn't take to strangers."

Adolf looked at us both. I poured some water in my hand for him to lick.

"Please continue, Jack," Christian said.

"Your father asked me to take care of them until they were older. He wanted them to have, as he called it, a more or less normal life. Your father went to rest in his car and he passed away in his sleep. So they ended up coming with me, because I promised to look after them. Adam can verify everything I've told you."

Christian sat there nodding his head. "I see. So they came with you of their own free will, because that's what my father wanted."

"Yeah. That's the story."

"Jack, may I see Adam and Emma?"

I thought for a minute and decided, why not. "Sure, I think that's a good idea."

I asked Tommy to go find Adam and Emma. I didn't want to take Christian onto Tocabaga since I didn't know who he really was.

As we sat there waiting, making small talk, Christian said, "That's a nice dog. What's his name?"

"Thanks. His name is Adolf."

"Is this the only way onto this island?"

"Yes, unless you come by boat."

"How many men do you have guarding this island?"

"Christian, I can't tell you that because of security reasons. Why do you wanna know?"

"I'd like to make sure that Adam has the necessary protection."

"Believe me, he does. Adam and Emma are living with my family."

Just then they came running over the bridge. Out of breath Adam said, "Hi Grandpa. You wanted to see us?" Emma gave me a big hug.

"Kids, do you know who this is?"

Both stared Christian and replied, "No."

"This is your uncle. He's your father's brother. His name is Christian de Molay."

Christian said, "That's right, I'm your uncle. Have you ever heard of me?"

"Yes, Grandpa spoke of you. He said you moved away and wouldn't be back," Adam replied.

"Yes, that's correct, but I'm back now. I'm the new Grand Master."

"Since you never came back, Grandpa told me I would be the next Grand Master when I'm sixteen."

"Adam, you're a little too young to be the Grand Master. That's my job now."

Little Emma just stood there not saying a word. She didn't know what to say about the subject. She had no idea what to think about Christian.

"I'm back now and I've come to rescue you both," Christian said.

Adam asked, "Rescue us from what?"

"You don't belong here. You need to be with your own people."

"Well, that's not want Grandpa wanted. God told him that we should go with Jack Gunn. He told me Jack would protect us until we're older. We like it here."

Christian let out a chuckle. "Adam, I'm your lawful uncle. It's my job to protect you, not Mr. Gunn's."

Adam looked directly in his eyes. "I'm sorry, but you're a stranger to us."

"I know that and I hope to get to know you both better. I need you both in my life. You're the only family I have now."

Adam and Emma moved closer to me. They were standing by my side with Adolf next to them.

Christian moved closer to the kids. Getting down on one knee he softly said, "Come here, my children," while holding out his open arms.

Adolf didn't like that and let out a low growl warning him.

I butted in, "Look Christian, the kids don't know you."

"Yeah, and we certainly aren't going to leave with you," Adam said.

Christian stood up and rested his hand on the broadsword, which made Adolf growl again.

"I see. I need to gain your trust," Christian

commented. "Jack, what do you suggest?"

It was a real dilemma, alright. If he's really their uncle, he has legal custody. I can't prove that he is or isn't their long-lost uncle. Normally I can spot a lair in a few minutes. This guy was smooth, very smooth, and I think he's a little too polite.

"Christian, I need to think about this and talk to the kids."

"They're just kids. They don't have any say in the matter. This is between you and me," he replied, in a not so friendly tone.

I thought, *he just blew his cool, a little. Maybe I can push him to the edge. If he's really their uncle then he'd want to consider what's best for them. He'd care about their wellbeing and safety.*

I said, "Christian, it's not between you and me. It's what's best for the kids. It's their future and they should have a say in what happens to them."

"I'm not going to change my mind. I'm their uncle and they need to come with me."

"That's not going to happen," Adam blurted out while pointing his finger at Christian.

"Look, it's getting late so let me talk to the

kids tonight," I said.

Christian asked, "Do you have some accommodations for me and my men?"

"I'm sorry, we don't. But you're welcome to camp on the beach, outside the fence tonight."

Christian stood up and bowed. "Until tomorrow. Children, I bid you a good night. Pack your clothes and be ready to leave tomorrow."

As he turned to walk away, he made a casual comment. "Adam, by the way, do you have the Grand Master's Sword?"

"Yes, I do."

"Ok. I just wanted to know who had it. Goodnight, kids. I'll see you tomorrow."

I said, "If you need anything just ask one of my guards."

"Thank you." He turned and walked away.

I told the kids, "Let's go home." Adam took Adolf's leash from my hand and they ran over the bridge to my truck.

Emma yelled, "Hurry up, Grandpa!"

Before leaving, I advised my security people

not to let any of these men inside the fence. Give them anything they need as long as it's within reason. If there's any problem, call me right away.

We arrived home and supper was almost ready. After eating, I called a family meeting to discuss the complicated situation. It was just Hemmi and I with the two kids. Emma sat on Hemmi's lap as we talked.

I asked, "Do you kids like it here?"

They both nodded. Adam replied, "We love it here. Don't make us go with my uncle. We don't know him."

"Is he really your uncle? Have you ever seen his picture?"

Emma shook her head yes. Adam said, "Yes, we've seen his picture. He's my uncle alright. At first I didn't know who he was because of the long beard."

We sat there quiet for a few minutes. I didn't know what to do or say to the kids. Their uncle does have a legal right to take custody of the children. I just wondered why he came for them after all these years.

I asked, "Adam, why did he ask you about the sword?"

"Whoever is the Grand Master gets that sword. It's been in our family a thousand years."

"Wow, so it's pretty valuable."

"Yes, it is."

I looked at Adam. "Is that why he wants it?"

Adam hesitated for a minute. "Yes, he came here to get the sword."

"Why do you think that?" Adam was hiding something. I had to pry information out of him. He started to fidget. "Look, Adam, I need to know everything to help you. We shouldn't have any secrets between us."

Emma said, "Tell Grandpa the truth."

"Well, the truth is, to become the real Grand Master you must have the sword. But there's another more important reason," Adam said, as he looked at me. "I'll tell you if you promise not to tell anyone else."

I replied, "Ok, Adam. You have my word."

"Come up to my room. I need to show you something."

Emma and Hemmi stayed on the patio while we went upstairs to his bedroom. After walking in the room, he closed and locked the door. He said, "What I'm about to show you is the most amazing secret you'll ever see. Only a few people know about this."

I said, "Don't worry; your secret is safe with me."

Adam stood there next to his bed and took a deep breath. "Ok."

He reached under his mattress and pulled out a wooden box. I remembered that the box contained a sword. Opening the box he took out the old broadsword. The scabbard looked old. The handle or grip was inlaid with gold and contained embedded rubies. The pummel had a golden cross on it. Holding the sword in both hands he kissed the handle and then pulled the big blade out of its scabbard.

"This is the Sword of Jerusalem." Adam said.

It was a beautiful looking weapon. The long blade almost glowed as he held it up in the air. It was shiny and looked like new. I was amazed by what I saw. Adam gently laid the sword on the bed.

"Here, look at this," Adam said, while pointing at the sword. "But don't touch the blade.

The rubies in the handle are a symbol for the blood of Christ."

I bent over and closely observed the blade. Some kind of foreign writing was etched in the metal blade. "What does it say?" I asked.

Adam didn't reply. He turned the sword over, showing the opposite side. There was more writing and a map etched into the metal. Adam said, "This is why he really wants this sword."

The map was so tiny I couldn't make it out with my bad eyesight. I couldn't read the writing because I didn't know the language it was written in. "Ok, I give up. What does it mean?" I asked.

Adam turned the sword back over to show me the text. "This writing lists all the items in the Templar Treasure." Turning the blade back over, he pointed at the map. "This map shows the location of the treasure."

I asked, "Do you mean the treasure items taken from Jerusalem?"

"Yes. I told you before, these are holy items. These items were once in the Temple of Solomon. They prove there is a God and there was a Christ. Men have killed each other for a thousand years to find this treasure."

"Holy crap." That was all I could say while glaring at the magnificent sword.

It was amazing. Now I knew the treasure was real, according to the sword and Adam. I commented, "Let me get this straight. If you have this sword, then you can find the treasure."

"That's correct. This is why we can't let Christian obtain this sword. No evil man should be in control of God's Treasure. I fear my uncle would use it to gain power and wealth."

"Why do you think he'd do that?"

"Well, Grandfather told me that Christian was outcast from the Knights Templar years ago because he tried to steal the sword. Grandfather also believed that Christian killed my father so he could become the next Grand Master in order to obtain the sword."

I nodded my head and thought, *this thing has turned into a very big and dangerous mess.*

I said, "If that's true then we certainly can't let your uncle take custody of you."

"It's true, alright. Grandpa would never let him near us."

"Didn't you tell me you saw the treasure

once?"

"Actually, I've never seen it, but I know it's real because of this sword."

I pointed at the sword. "Can you read this writing?"

"Yes, I know exactly what it says. Grandpa taught me. He could read the ancient Latin writing."

A light went off in my head. "Now I get it. Christian needs you to tell him what the sword says."

"Yes, I think you're correct," Adam said. "What are we going to do?"

I didn't reply right away. I had to think about this. Certainly, if this whole story is true then I can't let Christian obtain the sword, or Adam. The question is, if I don't give him what he wants, then what will Christian do?

Adam was looking at the sword as I put my hand on his shoulder. "Don't worry Adam. I'm not gonna let Christian take you or the sword. I promise you that."

Adam gave me a hug. "Thank you, Grandpa." We hugged each other and chills ran down my spine. Goosebumps popped up on my skin as I thought about the Power of the Sword and the secrets it held.

We stood there looking at the blade. Adam said, "You're the only one I can trust, other than Emma. Would you like to know what the writing means?"

I thought for a minute. "Only tell me if you really want to."

"I have to tell someone who's trustworthy, just in case something happens to me."

We bent over the sword. Pointing at the words he said, "This Sword is gifted to the Knights Templar Grand Master by Baldwin the Second, King of Jerusalem. Year of our Lord 1120 A.D."

"That's incredible," I murmured.

"The treasure contains: one hundred thousand gold coins, fifty thousand silver coins, five hundred golden goblets, one thousand silver goblets, twenty thousand pieces of gold and silver jewelry, ten thousand various pieces of art, and twenty thousand gold crosses."

"Is that all it says?" I asked.

"No. Now, for the good stuff. It says, the Holy Lance, the Sangreal, and the Ark of the

Covenant are part of the treasure. There's a date …
1124 A.D., Year of Our Lord."

I touched Adam on the arm. "If this is real
and the Ark of the Covenant is part of the treasure,
that's amazing. No one knows what type of power
the Ark has. I wonder if the Ten Commandment
tablets are inside?"

"It doesn't say what's inside the Ark."

"The main story about the Ark is that when
Jerusalem was invaded it was taken to Ethiopia. No
one has seen it since. Does the writing mention
that?" I asked.

"No, it only lists the treasure items." Adam
flipped the sword over. "Now, let me show you the
map. It also gives clues as to the location because
the map is not very telling."

I pulled out my reading glasses and looked
at the blade. There was a map that showed a river
and what looked like some mountains. There was a
hooked X marking the treasure location.

Adam began to ramble, telling me a long
story, about the Templars history.

"The Knights Templar were founded in
1118 by Hughes de Payen. This occurred after they
had a meeting with King Baldwin II, the King of

Jerusalem. His older brother was Godfroi de Bouillon who led the crusaders to victory in the Holy Land twenty years earlier.

"The Knights offered themselves as an order that would protect the roadways for pilgrims journeying to Jerusalem. They were given an entire wing of the royal palace for their headquarters. The wing had been built upon the foundations of Solomon's Temple. They received their name 'The Knights of the Temple.' Their real mission was to excavate the tunnels under Solomon's Temple looking for the treasure.

"In 1129, the Roman Catholic Church endorsed them as Holy Warriors and the protectors of Christendom. The Templars' reputation for bravery was well known. They were not allowed to retreat from battle and were obliged to fight to the death. They were also pledged to secrecy about the workings of the order."

"That's very interesting, Adam."

"Oh, there's a lot more, but I'll tell you later."

"Now, tell me about this map?"

Adam stared at the sword. "I'll explain the clues as best as I can.

"Upon arriving at the new land, sail south along the coast. Follow the coast which turns north, where the water is warm. Sail north, along the coast until you reach a great river that flows from the north.

"Sail up the great river for three days. Land at the point on the west bank marked by a stone cross where another great river mergers. The cross will point the way.

"Proceed west on the cross marked native trail for 40 days until reaching the stone trees. Beware of hostile natives along the way.

"Follow the cross west for another eight days to the rock castle.

"Go north for 15 days on the marked trail to a fissure in the earth. Here at the head of the trail, leading into the fissure, look for the cross and the Solstice sun will light the way.

"Signed by, Jacques de Molay, Grand Master 1306."

I said, "This means the Templars came here in 1300 which was way before Columbus."

"Columbus was actually searching for the treasure," Adam replied. "Do you have any idea where the treasure might be hidden based on this map?"

"No. I though you knew where it was."

"Grandpa tried to find it over the years, but he never did."

"We need a real map to see if we can determine what these clues mean. Back in those days the country was crisscrossed with Indian trails. The American Indians traveled by foot and took the most direct path. It appears that the Knights used the Indian paths. Many of our modern highways followed those trails."

"Yeah, that makes a lot of sense," Adam replied.

"I think that's enough for today. We'll work on this tomorrow. Right now, let's go tell Hemmi and Emma that you're staying here."

I was really interested in cracking the clues to find the treasure location. Actually going there to find it would be another problem, but the thought did intrigue me.

As Hemmi and I got ready for bed, I told her, "Tomorrow I'll tell Christian that Emma and Adam are going to stay here. I don't know what he'll do."

Hemmi said, "Don't take any chances. Kill him if you have to, but the kids stay here." Hemmi has never told me to kill anyone. I could tell she was dead serious, so to speak.

"Honey, I don't think it's gonna come down to that. Don't worry, everything will be fine."

I didn't want to tell her the truth, but deep down I thought it might come down to killing Christian.

As I dozed off, I made a plan to deal with Christian.

SEPTEMBER 14, 2025

Waking up, I was not looking forward to having a conversation with Christian. I gathered my key men for a meeting and I advised them of the situation. Christian was the kid's real uncle and did have the right to legal custody. The only reason he wanted them was because he wanted the sword.

Mike said, "Give him the sword and maybe he'll be happy and leave with no trouble."

I replied, "There's more to it than that. The sword is the key to finding the Templar treasure. Clues and a map are etched into the blade in ancient Latin. He needs Adam to translate it."

"Give him the sword and the translation, but not Adam," Tommy commented.

"Do you believe that crap about the Templar treasure?" Mike asked.

"Ok, here's the story. Adam's grandfather told him, that Christian killed his real father in order to be the next Grand Master. I fear Christian will kill Adam after he gets what he wants. Adam should be the next Grand Master when he's sixteen."

Chris asked, "What's in the treasure?"

"There's a fortune worth millions. But more importantly, it contains the Ark of the Covenant."

Mike laughed. "Now I know your bullshitting me."

"Mike, I'm just telling you what's written on the sword. I don't know if the Ark is there or not. To tell you the truth, I don't really wanna know. On the other hand, if the Ark is really there, we can't let any evil people obtain it. Who knows what could happen."

Tommy replied, "So we have to protect the sword and Adam. What do you want us to do?"

"I guess we got no choice," Mike blurted out.

"Thanks for your enthusiasm, Mike. Remember, we're doing this for the kids and for mankind. We're protecting God's Treasure.

"Here's my plan. Mike and Tommy, I want you both on sniper over-watch. They have four Hummers with machine guns. Your job is to take out the gunners. They have a total of 24 men. Shoot the others after you make sure their fifties are out of action.

"Chris, you and Carlos will man our Hummer guns. When you hear our snipers open up, bring the Hummers over the bridge and terminate anyone who doesn't surrender.

"Ron you make sure all our guards on the bridge are aware of what's going on so they can take cover and open fire when the shooting starts."

Mike asked, "What are you gonna do, Jack?"

"I'm gonna kill Christian if I have to. When I shoot him that'll be the signal to open fire."

"Tommy asked, "What are you gonna do, just walk up and shoot him in the face?"

"That's exactly what I'm going to do, if he gives me any shit. First, I'm gonna try to reason with him. I hope he'll leave in a friendly manner."

"What time is this going down?"

"I was thinking noon. Anyone have any suggestions?" The room was silent. "Ok, if nothing else, be set up before noon. I'll meet Christian exactly at noon. Remember, don't shoot until you see me shoot Christian."

The meeting broke up at 10 am. Everyone went to get ready for the possible battle. As I sat there, Adam walked in and gave me a hug. "Grandpa, I heard everything. I don't want you to get killed protecting me."

"Adam, don't worry, I have to do this. You're part of my family. On Tocabaga we're all family. The one thing I do know is how to protect my family. Besides, I think God is on our side."

"More than you may think, Grandpa."

My radio hissed. "Jack, you better come down to the fence. Christian de Molay is demanding to talk to you and Adam."

I checked my watch; it was only 10:30. "Ok, I'll be right there."

Adam said, "Don't go."

"You stay here with Adolf and I'll go see what he wants." I left the dog with Adam so he wouldn't be a distraction during a possible gun battle.

Twenty minutes later, taking my time, I approached the fence. Christian yelled, "Where the hell is Adam?"

Peering through the wire mesh I said, "Calm down. He just woke up."

He grabbed the fence and shook it. "I told you, I'm not leaving here without Adam. I told him to be ready to leave today!"

"It's not that easy. The kids don't wanna leave here. We discussed it last night."

"Bring Adam here right now! I wanna talk to him."

Looking directly into his eyes, I softly told him, "My friend, that's not gonna happen."

Christian let out a yell and shook the fence like a mad man. Now I knew he was just another big bully. Bullies try to get their way by intimidation.

"Jack, I'm warning you! I'll release fire and brimstone on you."

"Is that a threat?" I calmly asked, as I pulled out a smoke.

"It's a promise. If you don't bring Adam here in 15 minutes then we're going to have trouble."

"Look, I'm trying to reason with you. Your father wanted it this way. According to him, so did God. The kids are safe here."

Christian replied, "Here's what I suggest. You keep Emma, and Adam comes with me. Does that sound fair?"

I laughed in his face. "Christian, I know what you want. Adam told me last night. So cut the bullshit. If you think I'd let Adam and the sword go with you then you're crazy."

Christian grabbed the fence again and shook it like a crazed gorilla. "You're really pissing me off, Jack! If I get my hands on you, you're dead meat. Open the damn gate! Come out and fight me like a man. No weapons, just good old hand-to-hand combat."

Blowing a white cloud of smoke in his face, he backed away from the fence and coughed. I asked, "Why in the hell would I do that?"

"You're a coward, a chicken shit. You know I could beat your ass."

"You just don't get it. This isn't about you and me. It's about the kids and perhaps the future of mankind."

Christian's men were gathering behind him. They had their weapons in low ready position. They could kill me and maybe some of my men and storm the gate. All they needed to do was smash through it with the Hummers.

I was trying to buy some time until my men

were in position. It was only 11:20 so I had to stall him as long as possible.

Christian asked, "What do you mean the future of mankind?"

"The way I see it, if you get hold of the treasure, then the future of mankind is at risk."

"How do you know about the treasure?"

"Adam told me everything, including the fact that you tried to steal the sword and killed your brother. That's why you were outcast from the Knights Templar."

"That's a fucking lie! He was killed by someone during a home break-in."

One of his men walked up and asked Christian, "Is that true?"

"Yeah, he was killed when someone broke into his house, so shut the fuck up."

I replied to the solider, "That's not what Adam told me. Christian tried to steal the sword."

I heard a commotion behind me. I turned to see Adam walking towards me wearing a white mantle with the red cross on it. The sword was strapped on his waist.

I asked, "What are you doing?"

Adam answered, "I can't let you fight over the sword. I've decided to give it to Christian."

"Now you're talking kid," Christian commented. "Bring it here now."

Adam walked up to the fence peering at Christian. "I'll give you the sword under the condition that Emma and I stay here."

Big Christian thought about it for a minute. "It's a deal, if you tell me what the sword says."

"Ok, I agree."

I said, "Adam, wait don't agree to that."

"I have too. Please open the gate."

I nodded and opened it. Adam stepped outside with me by his side. I flicked my safety off as we walked out into the danger zone. I was prepared to kill Christian on the spot.

Adam stepped up, onto a foot high rock, near Christian. Christian and his men were watching his every move. Gazing at the warriors, he shouted in a firm voice, "My name is Adam de Molay. I'm the rightful heir to be the next Grand Master."

In one swift movement, he pulled the sword

out of its scabbard, kissed the ruby handle, and pointed it at the sky. Holding the blade high in the air, Adam shouted, "This is the Sword of Jerusalem! It holds the secrets to God's Treasure."

The blade was glowing in the bright sun. It reflected the sunlight like a mirror. Christian's soldiers all dropped to one knee. One man shouted, "Praise God!" They all repeated the words in unison and bowed their heads.

Christian saw his men all drop to one knee and so did he, right in front of Adam, a couple of feet away. With Christian's head slightly bowed I saw the sword reflect the sunlight over him.

Quickly and unexpectedly the sword flashed a white blinding light as if it was hit by a lightning bolt. A strong gust of wind blew up at the same time. The odd thing was, there was no noise. It was dead silent. I had to glance away and close my eyes from the intense flash of light. It was so strong, I could only see white spots for a second or two.

Opening my eyes, I looked up at Adam holding the sword. Blood was running down the blade. I realized what had just happened when I noticed Christian's head on the ground. His body, slumped over, was pumping blood out of his open neck.

Adam pointed the sword at the sky as crimson red ran down the shimmering blade. He said, "Glory to God in the highest."

The soldiers keenly looked at Adam and all repeated, "Glory to God." They all stood and bowed to him.

I wondered what just happened. Was that an act of God? Did God move Adam's arm to behead Christian? Was God actually using the sword to protect his treasure? Did Adam plan this all along? Invisible forces were at work for sure.

Adam kissed the handle, wiped the blood off on his white robe, and sheathed the blade. As Adam stepped down from the rock, he slumped to the ground. I jumped to help him back on his feet. He looked dazed and confused.

I kept an eye on Christian's men, not knowing what they would do. Then one man stepped forward towards Adam. I pointed my gun at him.

Holding his hands up he stopped and said, "Have no fear. My name is George Baldwin, Captain of these warriors. We're at your command,

Adam de Molay. Since you are the real Grand Master, we vow to follow your orders."

Now I knew things would never be the same. Adam had become Grand Master by the Power of the Sword. Now he had his own warriors to do God's work.

Adam said, "Thank you Captain Baldwin. I'll need your help and support."

I stepped up and shook Baldwin's hand. "I'm Jack Gunn, Director of Security for Tocabaga."

"It's a pleasure to meet you," George replied.

I said, "Since Adam is under my protection, I need to know your intentions."

"I understand your concern. We're Templar Warriors who do God's work. It was clear to us that God terminated Christian by working his will through Adam. There is no doubt that Adam has the Power of the Sword and God is on his side.

"As for my men, we were all once Marines

before becoming enlightened by God. Most of us saw combat in the middle-east fighting ISIS. After that we decided to do the Lord's work and became his warriors."

"Captain, Jack Gunn is my guardian and you will receive your orders from him and myself," Adam advised.

Baldwin nodded his head. "Yes sir. I understand."

Tommy and Mike came running up and saw Christian's head. "Holy crap. What happened?" Tom asked.

I replied, "I don't know. Get some men over here and remove the body."

Tommy had a puzzled look on his face. He then signaled for a few men to remove the body. As they picked up the body, Adam said, "I'd like him to be buried at sea. I'll speak at his funeral."

"Captain, please wait here with your men while I talk to Adam," I said.

I put my arm around Adam and we walked up the bridge. I asked, "What just happened?"

Adam stopped walking and faced me. "It was one of God's Angels that killed Christian, not me. God told me in a dream to take Christian the sword. He told me how to hold it. God told me not to fear for my life because he would protect me. When the bright light hit the sword, the angel took control of my body. I don't even know what happened."

"Adam, that's incredible. I seen a lot of stuff in my life, but I've never seen anything like that."

"Yes, it was a miracle. You believe in miracles, don't you?"

"Yes. I've had several prayers answered by God that could be considered a miracle. The most important one was when God saved Tommy from being a paraplegic."

We continued walking back to the house. I think Adam needed some rest.

Adam said, "Tell me about the miracle."

"Well, to make a long story short, when Tommy was fifteen, he was one of the leading male gymnasts in the country. One day, while doing a simple back-flip during practice, he landed on his neck. He complained of a lot of pain in his neck. His coach said we should have a Doctor look at him just to be safe, so he called the best-of-the-best doctor for sports medicine in area, just to have him checked out. He was a doctor who worked on pro football players and baseball players. We didn't think it was anything very serious, just a sprained neck.

"We went there and they took X- rays. In those days, that was all they could do, as there were no MRI's or modern technology like now. The Coach, my Son, and I sat there waiting for the X-ray results in the Doctor's office. After about an hour the Doctor came in and told us, 'I have bad news you. Your boy will never do any type of sports again. He has permanently damaged the ligaments between the 1st and 2nd vertebra. Any head motion could cause the upper spine to touch the spinal cord and he could become a paraplegic.' We couldn't believe it. It was a shock. "

"Gee whiz. That sounds pretty bad," Adam commented.

"The Doctor told him he must wear a metal neck brace, possibly forever, if he didn't want to be crippled. We were all stunned by the Doctor's bluntness.

"I ask the Doctor are you sure, are you positive, because it seems impossible that little fall could do that kind of damage. The Doctor said he had two other Orthopedic Doctors confirm his results. The only other way to confirm it would be by doing surgery but the damage couldn't be repaired. So why risk the surgery.

"So what did you do?" Adam asked.

"That night, I prayed; we all prayed for this nightmare to go away. I prayed everyday for some answer or something to make this a better situation. I never prayed so much in my life. This thing haunted me and we needed God's help. But God helps those that help themselves. I made a pact, an agreement, with God that if he helped my Son, I would never ask him for another thing for myself.

"I started calling every Doctor in the phone book. I found four new Doctors and we went to each one over the next three months. The answer was the same: keep your brace on because it will never get better. Three long months had gone by with no hope in sight.

"Three months is a long time to wear a brace," Adam commented.

"One day at work, I was talking to a friend of mine about what happened and he advised me the name of a scoliosis doctor. I called his office and to my surprise, his secretary put him on the phone right away. Dr. Brown told me to bring in the X-rays and my Son the next day. Dr. Brown looked at the X-rays and then took more X-rays and did some

71

testing. I was sitting there praying the whole time.

"They came back into the office and Dr. Brown looked at me and said, 'I have good news.' Dr. Brown stated that there was nothing wrong with him. His neck was fine and he should take off the brace and start on an exercise program for a month before going back into gymnastics.

"I asked, are you sure? Brown advised he was 100% sure. He also gave me the name and phone number of the leading specialist in the country located in New York City.

"Dr. Brown showed us the X-rays he took and the ones taken before. There was a clear difference. He told us maybe the original X-rays weren't taken correctly or … maybe it was a miracle. It was a miracle for sure."

Adam said, "Wow, that's a great story. See, that's the power of prayer. So you haven't asked God for anything else?"

"I've never asked God for anything other than to protect us when we go into battle. I also ask him to watch over my family."

When we arrived home, Emma and Hemmi gave Adam a hug. They had already heard, through the grapevine, what happened to Christian.

I asked Adam, "What are we gonna do with the Templar warriors?"

Adam said, "Captain Baldwin is a descendant of King Baldwin of Jerusalem. God has a plan for him. Can you house the warriors here for a while?"

"Yeah, but can we trust them?"

"Yes, we can. I'm one hundred percent sure of that."

"Ok. I'll put them up in the high and dry for now until we find something better. We'll have to check them all for Ebola before they move in, and give them a background check.

"How do you know he's related to King Baldwin?"

Adam said, "God told me that Baldwin would enter my life. If you don't mind I need to rest now."

I was worried about Adam and took him up to his bedroom. "Adam, are you OK?"

"Yes. I just need to rest. All my energy is gone."

"Ok, if you need me just call." He put the

sword under his mattress and I kissed him on the head. As I walked out of the room, he got on his knees and started to pray.

I wondered how he knew that an angel killed Christian. After what happened today I'll pretty much listen to whatever Adam tells me. He's made me a believer that God talks to him.

Heading back to the bridge, I had Chris check the 24 warriors for Ebola. Mike ran a quick background check and they were all cleared. We moved them into the high and dry, leaving the Hummers and trucks in the parking lot.

Tommy, Mike, and I sat around with a few of my other men getting familiar with the Templars. They seemed like honest men who wanted nothing more than to serve God and country. I liked them and so did Tommy.

Since Tommy was a Marine sniper once, they had a lot in common. They all seemed to know who Tommy was and he had heard about a few of them. The meeting made me feel a lot better about these men.

Baldwin gazed at the ring on my finger. "Are you a Seal?" he asked.

I held up my hand showing the ring. "No.

This belongs to my friend, Rico Martin." I proceeded to tell them the story about Rico, and the run in we had with Dirty Dan.

Baldwin replied, "So you guys have seen some action around here. It sounds to me like we need to get rid of this Dirty Dan."

"That's easier said than done," I said.

"Jack, that's our specialty. Sneak, peek, and assassinate the bad guys."

Baldwin was a bruiser of a man, standing about six two and I'd guess around 230 pounds. He had a rough looking face with a scar that ran down the entire left side. To sum it up, he appeared to be one tough dude. I liked him right off the bat.

Mike said, "We're glad you guys are here, but we need Mr. Dirty alive to find out where Rico is."

"We can do that, also."

Looking at Baldwin, I said, "Let's discuss that tomorrow. Adam tells me you're related to King Baldwin, was the first Christian King of Jerusalem."

"Yes, that's correct. Most of us are related to original Templars in some manner. We're a band of brothers."

All his men shouted in unison, "Oorah!"

"That's very interesting. It explains a lot of things. But why did you hook up with Christian?"

George Baldwin glanced around at his men. "I think everyone here would agree that he conned us." His men nodded in agreement. "He proved to us who he was, and told us that his nephew, Adam, was keeping the Sword of Jerusalem for him. After arriving here, we all sensed there was a problem. We suspected he was trying to steal it from Adam."

"He was gonna steal it, and possibly do harm to Adam." I stood up and stretched my legs. "George, don't you think Adam is a little too young to be the Grand Master?"

George stood up next to me and put his hand on my shoulder. "My friend, age doesn't matter. He's being led by God. King Baldwin the fourth was made king at the age of sixteen."

"Yeah, I guess you're right. But he's just a kid to me. Hey, Why don't we all get a beer and we'll give you a tour of the island. Tomorrow we'll find you guys some decent quarters."

After a brief tour, we were sitting around the bar in the Green Room. Tommy asked, "George, how did you guys meet Christian?"

George replied, "In the Marines. We worked with him for a while. Then when we got out he arranged a security job for us working at the Lima Tank Plant in Ohio. We did that for a few years until the collapse of the government. The plant closed and we kept our equipment. We confiscated the Humvees and trucks before anyone could steal them. Then we started purging the country of ISIS, drug gangs, and other radicals."

As George took a swig of water, I asked, "So who told you Adam was here?"

"That's a good question. Every now and then Christian would receive a phone call from a guy named Canfield. I don't know who he is, but he would tell Christian what was going on with the Molay Order and how his father was doing."

I thought about what George just told me. "Sounds to me like this guy Canfield is a spy."

Baldwin nodded in agreement. "But we didn't know it at the time. Christian led us to believe that we would join the main group after his father had passed. Then he would become the Grand Master. So we followed him just doing a job riding the country of scum bags."

"So this guy, Canfield, told Christian that Adam was here."

"Yeah. One day he received a phone call. It was right after the Arctic Vortex hit up north. Christian told us to pack up we were moving south to Florida. We liked that idea because it was getting damn cold up there."

I was trying to put two and two together. "Did Canfield call telling you that Jack de Molay was dead?"

George thought for a minute before replying. "Yeah, he must have called Christian because he knew right where the grave was located on the side of the road."

"Ok, this makes a lot of sense. Canfield had to be in that group of Templars. But how did you know we were here on Tocabaga?"

Tommy spoke up, "Someone probably followed us here."

I took a sip of whiskey and scratched my chin. "You're right. Someone followed us here. George, do you know where the other Templars are located?"

"I only know they're somewhere near here."

"Well, I know where they are. Hey, what happened to Christian's phone?"

Everyone looked around at each other. Tommy replied, "Oh, I got it."

I said, "Good, hang on to that phone. It'll have Canfield's number on it, which proves he's the spy that phoned Christian. If it rings, don't answer it. Tomorrow I'm gonna ask Adam if he knows Canfield."

"That's a good idea," Tommy stated.

I asked, "George, are you going to stay here on Tocabaga?"

Baldwin and his men looked at me. "We hope so, if you'll have us. Our job is to protect the Grand Master and follow his orders."

"Speaking for myself and my men, we'd like you to stay. I'll officially introduce you to the community tomorrow. I don't think anyone will object."

"That sounds great." Baldwin said with a smile.

The party broke up and everyone retired for the night. I warned Baldwin and his men not to roam around outside the boat storage area because of our K-9 patrols. Someone might shoot them by mistake.

     I went home and found everyone was asleep, except for Adolf. I sat down and had a smoke before going to bed. It had been a crazy day to say the least. I felt good about the Templars being here and was pretty sure we could trust them. Tomorrow I'd have to think of some way to prove it. I didn't trust anyone. They needed to earn my trust.

SEPTEMBER 15, 2025

After breakfast, Tom and I were discussing the Templar warriors, who were parked in the high and dry for now. Tom seemed convinced that they were stand-up guys. Tom commented, "I asked them a lot of questions about the Marines and what they did in the Middle East. They're the real deal, alright."

I asked, "Do you think they could capture Dirty Dan?"

"Capture … I'm not sure, but I know they could bump him off."

Adam walked in the room. I asked, "Adam do you know a man named Canfield?"

"Yes, Mr. Canfield. He's the one that tried to take us the night Grandpa died. Why?"

"He's a spy who was working for Christian. That's how Christian found you. He had someone follow us here."

"Gee, how do you know that?"

The radio came on. "Jack, come down to the fence right away. That Freddy guy is back," Chris said.

Tommy said, "I wonder what that jerk wants?"

"God works miracles in many ways," I replied. "Let's see what the hell he wants this time. Adam, I'll get back to you later; this is an urgent matter."

Arriving at the fence, Freddy was sitting on the ground. He looked like shit. Freddy had been worked over pretty good. His face was swollen. His nose was broke and one eye was puffed up. He looked in damn bad shape; bleeding from his ears and nose.

Opening the gate, Tommy told him to stand up. He was barely able to stand. Tommy frisked him for weapons. Freddy said, "I don't have any guns."

"Alright, asshole, what do you want?" I asked.

"I got some news for you."

"Ok, spit it out."

"First of all, Dirty killed Reed for screwing up the gun deal. I barely escaped with my life. I didn't know where to go … so I came here for help.

I know you're a good guy."

"Yeah, yeah. What else you got."

"I can tell you where to find Dirty Dan."

I thought for a minute. "Why do you wanna do that?"

Freddy coughed up some bright red blood. "Cause … I want him dead."

"Tell me what happened to Rico."

"We found Rico … half alive off of 54th Avenue. He looked like a crispy critter. Rico asked us to bring him here … to you. Dan killed him, took his gun, knife, and ring. Then he dreamed up … the stupid plan … to get some guns from you."

"Where can we find Dirty?"

"He's at the big green house on 23rd Avenue. You can't miss it. Most of the gang hangs out there … with whores … taking drugs." Freddy could hardly speak; he was holding his chest. "Every night, exactly at midnight, Dirty goes across the street to the bar. You gonna … help me?" Freddy fell to his knees and laid on the ground. "I can't breathe."

I bent down on one knee close to him. Blood

was flowing out of his mouth and nose. "Freddy, I think you're hurt real bad. Your lung's collapsed. There's not much I can do to help you."

Freddy kept coughing up blood. As he closed his eyes, I could tell he was drowning in his own red fluid. I told him, "We'll kill Dirty Dan."

I heard the gurgle of his last bloody breath.

I stood up. Chris was next to me. "Fish food, Jack?"

I patted Chris on the back. "Yep, he's fish food."

As Tom and I walked away, I thought, *this is a chance for Baldwin to prove how good his men are.* As if reading my mind, Tommy said, "I'll set up a mission tonight with the Templars, to kill Dirty Dan."

I replied, "Make it so. At least we know what happened to Rico."

"Yeah. It's too bad we can't give him a proper send off."

"I wonder what became of his son and wife."

"I guess we'll never know for sure," Tommy

put his hand on my shoulder. I'll go with the Templars since I know the area. That way I can confirm the kill."

I nodded my head as we walked to the boat dock to bury Christian at sea. It was a brief service since the only one who spoke was Adam. He asked God to have mercy on Christian's soul. He said that Christian was possessed by the devil or demons. A couple of our anglers took his body out to sea.

Later that day, I found a map of the United States. Adam and I sat down to study it. We were looking for anything that could be related to clues on the sword.

"Where do we start looking?" Adam asked.

"I'm not sure," I replied, as my eyes wondered over the surface of the map.

After thirty minutes, Adam asked, "How do you think they sailed here without a map back in those days?"

"Yeah, that's it Adam. We have to go back to the beginning."

"What do you mean *the beginning?*"

"Well, maybe they did have a map of some kind. Years ago, the Vikings sailed here jumping across the Atlantic to Iceland and Greenland. We know they landed in Nova Scotia and traveled further south along the coast. Maybe the Knights took the same route using a Viking map."

"That makes a lot of sense because we know they sailed from somewhere in northern England," Adam advised.

"Ok, let's assume that they landed in Nova Scotia. The sword says follow the coast south until it turns north. I wonder what the heck that means?"

Adam corrected me. "To be exact the sword reads: Upon arriving at the new land, sail south along the coast. Follow the coast which turns north, where the water is warm. Sail north, along the coast until you reach a great river that flows from the north."

Squinting at the map I took a deep breath. "Adam, I need a smoke break. Besides, it's getting late and dinner is almost ready. You get washed up while I make my security rounds. We'll look at this tomorrow."

I walked over to the boat yard. Tommy was

there, along with Baldwin and his men, discussing the plan to kill Dirty. When I walked in, all the men stood-up and greeted me. I said, "Thank you for going on this mission."

Christian replied, "We can't let a junkie gangster get away with killing a Navy Seal. We didn't know Rico, but we're still his brothers."

Tommy said, "Here's the plan. We're taking all four Hummers with 16 men. We'll park them on Route 275 and then four of us will infiltrate to within 300 yards of the house at 23:00 hours. We'll have two shooters, me and Captain Baldwin. Our rifles will have silencers. The other two men will carry SAWs in case we have a run in with a large group of hostiles."

"Once we terminate the target, we'll extract the way we came in. The trucks will move in to pick us up, so we can make a fast exit," Baldwin advised.

"Captain, what are you shooting?" I asked.

"An M40A6 chambered for 7.62x51mm with night vision. I think it's the same as Tom's weapon."

"Ok, it sounds good to me. Don't take any unreasonable risks. May God be with you." I shook each man's hand and left.

As I walked back home, I had no doubt that Dirty Dan was as good as dead. I'm sorry to say, it made me feel good. An eye for an eye is what I always say.

My family sat down for dinner and the only one missing was Tom. Tonya, Tommy's wife, asked, "Jack, where's Tom at?"

"He's over with the Templars talking about old times. I think he'll be a while." I didn't wanna tell her the truth or she'd get pissed off. Lucky for me, she didn't ask any more questions.

Everyone went to bed, but I couldn't sleep knowing my son was out there in the danger zone. We always go on missions together and watch each others' back. Now he was with strangers, for the most part, so I was a little concerned about his safety.

After pouring a shot of JD, I lit up a smoke while sitting on the patio with Adolf. It was 12:30 am when the radio hissed, making me jump a little. "Dad, the target is terminated. Over."

"Roger that. Everyone alright?"

"No problems encountered. We'll be back soon."

"I'll buy y'all a drink. Over and Out."

I thought, *vengeance is mine saith the Lord. Well Lord, I had to help you out a little with this one. Do what you will with his soul.*

I still wondered what happened to Rico's wife and son. It bugged the hell out of me.

THOMAS H. WARD

SEPTEMBER 16, 2025

The termination team made it back ok. We went to the Green Room last night and all got a little drunk. It was a party for Rico.

It seems we can trust the Knights to keep their word, so I arranged for them to move into some empty condos near the bridge. After discussions with Mike, Tom, Rick, and Chris, we all felt it would be best if they became our roving police force. They could leave Tocabaga, enforce the laws, and help the needy. They could help find poor little kids running around out there with no food. Most importantly, they could cleanse our area of al-Qaida, ISIS fighters, gangs, and Free Roamers who may still be lurking around.

My plan was to introduce them to the community at the fire circle tonight. The community needed to know who these men were and what they were doing here. The problem was, I really didn't know exactly what to tell our community. Most people don't want any more strangers coming here to live because it drains our resources.

One benefit was we had a lot more fire power with the four additional Humvees. These men are very experienced warriors. They've seen everything and were battle hardened.

Tradition has it that we light the fire circle downtown at dusk. Most people go there to meet friends and exchange daily news. Of course, most of the news is gossip and not necessarily true. People can air their grievances and complaints, more or less, getting things off their chests.

It was almost dark as we arrived with the Templars at the meeting. One of the first people we meant was Maggie. She walked over to us with her shepherd, named Freda, on a leash. She shook each man's hand and let the dog smell them.

Maggie's husband was killed by the Fed's during one of our many encounters. She had been living by herself and hadn't dated anyone on the island. Maggie is a good friend and an excellent Amazon Warrior. I can trust her with my life and have done so many times.

I introduced her to Captain George Baldwin, the last man in line. "Maggie, this is Captain George Baldwin."

She replied, "Hello, Captain. It's a pleasure to meet you." Maggie was gazing into his eyes.

"Please call me, George."

I saw a smile come across her face. "Ok George, you can call me Miss Maggie."

They both laughed. "Ok, Miss Maggie."

"I'll let you call me Maggie after we get to know each other better." They both chuckled again. "I get off duty in two hours. How about we have a drink together?"

"That sounds good, Miss Maggie."

I was standing there thinking, *Maggie is finally gonna have a date.* She let it be known that she was single by using the word Miss.

"Ok, Captain, meet me at the Green Room. I'll be there by ten."

"Alright, I'll be there."

I butted in. "Ok, you guys. We got a lot of people to meet. Maggie, you gotta finish your patrol."

As we walked away, George and Maggie gazed back at each other. She had a stupid smile on her face and was putting on a sway. George said, "Jack, she's beautiful. Tell me about her."

"She's as deadly as she is beautiful. Maggie is one of my best fighters. She's a captain in my

Amazon Warrior clan."

"What are Amazon Warriors?"

People were walking up, introducing themselves to the Templars as George and I tried to carry on a conversation.

"The Amazon Warriors are a group of twenty women who I trained as fighters. They're more or less the police force here on the island."

"I noticed she carried a sword on her hip."

"That's not a sword, it's a machete. She knows how to use it. I was with her when she cut the head off a dirtbag."

"Wow, she cut a guy's head off?"

"Yep. She's one tough cookie. We went to this gang house to rescue a friend's wife. The gang leader was holding her there against her will. Anyway, to make a long story short, the dirt bag, named Buck, tried to grab Maggie and she cut off his hand. He dropped to the ground to pick up his hand and she wacked his head off in one blow.

"I'll finish the story later. It's time for me to say a few words to the people here." There was a crowd of about one hundred people present.

I introduced the Knights Templar warriors to the crowd. Adam was standing there with us. "Friends, I'd like to introduce you to the Templar Warriors. These men are here to help us. Adam is the new Grand Master of the Templars in case you haven't heard. These men will help provide us added security."

Jace, one of our trusted men, yelled, "Is it true that Adam killed one of them?"

I responded, "It was God's will. He was a traitor who killed Adam's father. That's all I have to say about it." The crowd was whispering back and forth to each other.

I spoke up right away, trying to change the subject, but a man named Malcolm interrupted. "We heard Adam used a sword and cut the guys head off. He killed him in cold blood."

Malcolm is one of our farmers. He's a little out spoken, but he means no harm. I replied, "Look, you weren't there. It was an act of God. A bright light came out of the sky and blinded everyone for a second. When we regained our vision his head was cut off. As weird as it sounds, Adam says he didn't kill Christian."

"If Adam didn't kill him; then who did?"

"Malcolm, do you believe in God?"

Malcolm hesitated for a moment. "No, not really."

"Then you can't understand what happened. It was one of God's Angels that killed him. He took control of the sword and did the deed."

"Oh come on, Jack. You expect us to believe that crap. You're just protecting the kid."

"Malcolm, I don't care what you believe. If you don't believe in God then you'll never understand what happened. So kindly sit down and let me finish the meeting."

Jace said, "Yeah Malcolm, sit down." Malcolm stormed out of the meeting along with a couple of other non-believers. Jace and Malcolm are always arguing about something, but they're still buddies. Jace works in the kitchen along with Rahim and Steve.

I continued, "The Templars are going to be our roving police force outside of Tocabaga. These men will be our eyes and ears to the outside world. My goal is to rid the area of junkies and Free Roamers. With daily patrols, we can clean up the area step by step. We'll be a lot safer."

Jace shouted, "Sounds good to me, Jack."

"I realize having these additional men here will present a little extra burden on our resources. We'll need to boost up food production to cover an additional twenty-four more men. Believe me; it's going to be well worth it."

I ended the meeting by advising the Templars would be roaming around the crowd to introduce themselves to everyone. Some people clapped and some just walked away. You can't please everyone.

Baldwin commented to me. "Thanks for the introduction. How many people live here?"

"There's a little over six hundred. We have about 120 who work security. The rest do what needs to be done to keep this place functioning. They fish, hunt, farm, and cook. We have garbage details, lawn cutting, general clean up, and so forth. Everyone chips in and does the normal maintenance work that's required."

Captain Baldwin pointing south towards No Man's Land asked, "What's on that other island?"

"Oh, that's where our farm is. Maggie is in charge of that along with two old farmers we rescued from the Feds a while back. It's also an Army Ranger base called Fort Desoto."

"Are there any Rangers there now?"

"No, not now. They're on a mission down south. Hey, it's getting late so Adam and I are going home. I'll see you tomorrow."

"Ok Jack, see you tomorrow. Thanks for making us feel at home here."

"No problem. Maggie will be getting off duty soon so just wait here for her."

Captain Baldwin bowed to Adam and they shook hands. As we walked home, I glanced around and saw the rest of the Templars were mixing in the crowd getting to know their new friends.

I felt bad for the people who didn't believe what happened to Christian was an act of God. I knew there was no way Adam could swing that sword hard enough to cut off a man's head.

Adam said, "The meeting went pretty good."

"Yeah, except for Malcolm butting in," I replied. I put my arm around his shoulder as we walked home. "You gotta remember not everyone believes in God, but that doesn't mean they're bad people. Malcolm is a good guy who would help just about anyone."

"I know, he's taught me a lot working out on

the farm. Now I know why God chose you to watch over us."

"Oh, why's that?"

"You're teaching me how to be tolerant of others."

I nodded. "Maybe you're right. Let's go take a look at that map again."

We studied that stupid map until Adam fell asleep.

THOMAS H. WARD

SEPTEMBER 17, 2025

Today we would make a plan or directive for the Knights to follow. Mike and I would go out on patrol with them on the first day to show them the area.

They would operate, more or less, like a police force. Many of the poor people living in the condo ruins had no other place to go. They were just trying to stay alive. It was the junkies and Free Roamers who were dangerous. They needed to be removed or terminated for our safety and the safety of any harmless people living there.

My goal was to help these people by giving them a secure place to live. I also wanted to provide them supplies and food. If they had their own seeds, they could grow food. If they had fishing gear, they could harvest fish. We needed to rebuild the area from the ground up. The key was to establish law and order first. This was right job for the Templars.

At least half of the condos had been destroyed over the past couple of years. There are approximately 120 buildings that will have to be searched one by one. It's a big job, but the Knight Warriors had the necessary experience.

In discussion with Captain Baldwin and his men, we decided to set up four five man squads. Each squad would have a Humvee with a fifty caliber, and two M249 machine guns. Everyone else would carry the M4 along with four M67 hand grenades.

The plan was to start clearing the buildings nearest the road on the south side. One squad would precede east and one squad west, clearing units one by one. Since the condo complex is on a circular island, the squads would meet on the north side. I estimated it would take about a week to secure the area.

The other two squads would provide security at east and west bridges, thereby closing the roads leading onto the island. They would stop any undesirables, but allow those to enter who seemed like normal families. Of course, these people would be interviewed.

To keep unwanted dirtbags from coming back at night, the Templars would block access around the clock. The remaining four warriors would be assigned to patrol the area at night. We also hoped that the people whom we helped would be our eyes and tell us if any undesirables did move back in.

My goal was to protect the decent law

abiding people. I wanted them to become our friends. I wanted them to be self-sufficient. To do this, we'd have to build a good rapport with the locals. It would be necessary to provide them food, tools, and knowledge.

Captain Baldwin and I thought the plan was a good one. Of course, if the Templars ran into any over whelming forces, our Tocabaga security would provide back-up for them.

By the time we finished making our plans, it was almost noon. After a bite to eat, we proceeded with our mission. While driving to the condos, Captain Baldwin asked, "How did these buildings get destroyed?"

"We've had a few battles here with the Feds, gangs, and al-Qaida. The Army had no choice but to blow the hell out of the buildings to kill the bad guys."

We stopped at the first building and I pointed. "You see the high grass and bushes here. You can't tell it now, but this used to be a nice golf course. Hidden in that jungle are a few small fresh water lakes. You gotta be careful in there. If you fall into one of those lakes you could become gator food."

Baldwin laughed a little. "You're joking, right?"

"No, it's not a joke."

Baldwin looked at me with a serious expression on his face. "I've never seen a gator close up."

We continued the tour around the condo island. When we finished, Baldwin ordered his men to set up security on the two bridges as planned. The other two squads started clearing buildings.

Mike and I watched them from our truck. The Templars were a well-oiled machine. Each man knew what to do. They cleared the first building in an hour, but found no people. If anyone resisted, they would be removed by force. If someone shot at us, then we'd have to use deadly force.

People who were co-operative would be taken aside and interviewed. The interview was to determine who these people really were and determine how we could help them. We were trying to improve their lives.

While sitting in the truck, I realized that even if we made this area safe, it would never be the same. It would take years to rebuild these condos and a lot of equipment that we didn't have. It was almost a hopeless cause. It was a fact that more and more people were moving here from the north. Local residents were moving back to their homes from the green zones. Soon we'd have a lot of people to deal with.

That could be good or bad. That's why it was necessary to establish law and order now. We couldn't wait for the Rangers to return.

Baldwin came out of the second building. He was carrying a woman in his arms. As he walked up to us, Mike and I jumped out of the truck to help him. She was an old woman who looked undernourished and sickly, perhaps she was in her eighties. Her clothes reeked of urine and feces.

George said, "I found this old lady lying in a bed next to her dead husband. Her name is Mrs. Jackson." I opened the Hummer rear door and Baldwin laid her in the back.

Mrs. Jackson cried, "They killed my husband. I can't live without him. I just wanna die."

I said, "Mrs. Jackson, we're gonna take care of you. We'll get you some food and medical help."

I took out a bottle of water and placed the rim to her lips while Mike held her up to take a drink. She took a couple of sips and I withdrew the bottle when she started to cough. It seems she had been without water for a few days. We were just in time to save her life.

"Can you bury my husband for me?"

"Yes, we'll take care of him, don't worry. Tell me who killed him?"

She could barely speak. "It was al-Qaida. When he tried to stop them from taking our food, they shot him."

"Where are these men now?" Mike asked.

"I think they live over in the main building. You know, the old club house."

I told her. "Mrs. Jackson, we're gonna take you to the clinic now." She laid her head back, closing her eyes, and didn't speak anymore. I wondered if she would make it. I wondered if she even had the will to live.

Mike took her to Doc. Scott, at our clinic, while I talked to Captain Baldwin. "We have to terminate these guys. I didn't know al-Qaida was living here."

The Captain replied, "Killing jihadists is what we do best."

George called over one of his men. "Pete, take Jeff and go over to the main building. Scout it out. See if you can locate these guys and find out how many are there. Be careful because they probably know we're here. Report back, ASAP."

"Roger that, boss," Pete replied. We watched Pete and Jeff jog away.

Pete and Jeff were Baldwin's go-to men. They were the most experienced of the group. You could tell the other Templars respected them and followed every order to the letter. Pete is a normal looking lanky guy, standing almost six feet tall. Jeff is stocky, with a thick neck and a large head. He moves like a cat.

George said, "As soon as they report back, we'll take care of these bad boys. It's pretty disgusting killing an old man for some food."

Baldwin pulled out his sword and ran his thumb down the blade. "It's sharp enough."

"Sharp enough for what?" I asked.

"Sharp enough to cut off a few heads."

"Are you really gonna do that?"

"Hell yeah. Jihadists are scared shitless to have their heads cut off. If they don't have a head they can't enjoy the virgins in heaven. No head is bad juju for them."

"I didn't know that."

"Yeah, it's true. If we take anyone alive, I'll cut all their heads off except for one. I'll let that man go free so he can go tell his friends what we did. They won't dare come around here anymore."

After scratching my head I said, "Or … maybe it'll piss them off and more of them will come here."

Baldwin shrugged his shoulders. "They're all cowards. But if they do come back, we'll kill them all. Don't worry; I know what I'm doing. I've been fighting these guys for years."

I sensed some tension between us. "I'm not worried, Captain."

"Good. I have to get back to my men and clear these buildings. You wanna come along?"

"Ok, let's go."

We arrived at the fifth condo building, which had five stories with four units on each floor. "Jack, watch what we do. You'll be the last one in line behind me. Your job is to watch our backs."

"Roger that. I stay by the door and cover our backs."

"Affirmative."

We cleared the fifth building and found two middle-aged men hidden on the top floor. They were armed when the Knights bashed in the door to their unit, but dropped their guns when they heard, 'U.S. Marines, drop your guns!' They obeyed the command and raised their hands.

Baldwin had told me ahead of time he was going to identify our group as U.S. Marines. I asked why and he told me, because it sends fear into the enemy. I couldn't argue with that comment. Who the hell wants to fight the Marines? After all, who's going to be afraid if we yell, 'Tocabaga Security'?

I took the two men outside at gunpoint to conduct an interview. I told them who I was and asked them to sit down. I kept my carbine pointed at them and started to ask them questions. "Who are you guys?" They were brothers, Bill and Ted Cramer. "Why are you guys living here?"

They seemed to be in pretty good shape, sporting full beards with long hair. They looked like

Free Roamers. I guessed them to be about thirty something. I found out they were preppers that have lived here for two years, under the radar so to speak.

Bill pleaded, "Please don't take our supplies."

I advised, "Don't worry, we're here to help you. No one's gonna steal anything."

George came outside and looked at the men. "Man, you guys got a lot of stuff up there." They nodded in agreement. "Where'd you get the AK47's from?"

Ted replied, "We bought those years ago."

George looked at Ted. "Those guns will get you killed."

"How's that? So far they've saved our lives."

"AK's are junk guns. They're not very accurate. I can jam one just by stomping on the receiver, by the ejection port."

"How long have you guys been living here?" Baldwin asked.

"Like, we told Jack, about two years. This used to be our parents place. When they passed away, we moved in."

"You know, there's radical Muslims living nearby. How come they haven't killed you?"

Both men laughed. "We can speak Arabic. They think we're Muslims. We give them stuff every now and then. They leave us alone for the most part."

"You look like Muslims. Where did you learn to speak Arabic?" I asked.

"Our Father was from Morocco. He moved here 40 years ago and married a Christian, our mother. Then he converted. We also studied Arabic in college."

"So are you Muslims'?"

They glanced at us and then at each other. Ted said, "No, of course not. We're Christians. You won't find any prayer rugs in our home."

Baldwin's radio hissed, "Boss, we got eyes on the J's [jihadists] and there's six that I can see. They're armed, alright."

"Roger that. Keep watching them for now. Over."

"Affirmative."

"Bill, how many jihadists are there?" Baldwin asked.

"I guess about six men and four women. We don't really know for sure. Oh, there's also some kids."

"Damn it anyhow, kids and women. That's all we needed to screw this up. We don't kill kids and women … unless we have to." Everyone looked at Baldwin. "What? Why are you looking at me? If they point a gun at you what are you gonna do?"

I said, "George, let's get the men together and make a plan to deal with these J's."

"I was getting to that. There's no hurry. They're not going anywhere."

George radioed his two teams to come in. We made a plan to assault the building. It was a simple plan, using the Humvee fifties, we would surround the building and give them a chance to surrender. If they didn't, then we'd blow them away. George felt sure they would rather surrender than risk their family getting killed in a fire fight.

The clubhouse or main building had locker rooms with showers. There was a dining room, kitchen, and a few office spaces. It was about 10,000 square feet in size.

We slowly encircled the one-story building. No one fired at us while doing so. We had the two Humvees and a total of eleven men, including me. Everyone was behind some type of cover. A tree, wall, or any protection that was handy and secure.

George pulled Bill over to his side. "I want you to repeat what I say in Arabic incase some of them don't understand English." He nodded ok. "U.S. Marines. Come out with your hands up! You're surrounded. Leave your weapons inside. You have five minutes before we start shooting." Bill shouted into the megaphone in Arabic. We hoped he was repeating exactly what George said, but we had no idea.

Four minutes had passed by and I was getting worried. Then the front door slowly opened and out stepped four women with three little kids, holding their hands in the air. One of them shouted, "No shoot, No shoot us!" Three women were dressed in traditional clothing, wearing the simple head scarves called the hijab, but one had on a dark blue burqa which covered her head and face.

George ordered them to sit in front of him in a straight line with their backs to us. Right away, I knew why he did that. If the men inside decided to fight, the women and children would be in the line of fire. They would be gunned down by their own people. Also, the women might have guns hidden on them. We had to keep any eye on the women.

Five minutes were almost up when one man stepped out. "Don't shoot," he said, in perfect English. Following behind him were the remaining five men with their hands in the air. Pete, Jeff, and George pulled each man aside and searched them for weapons. They were clean. The men all had on the traditional red and white checkered ghurta. George ripped the scarfs off their heads.

Pete and Jeff proceeded to zip tie their hands, behind them, so there was no chance they could do anything stupid. After they were all tied up, Captain Baldwin had his men go in the building and search it for anyone else. It was clear.

Baldwin had them all stand in a line while he walked up to each one, peering at their faces. Coming over to me, Baldwin whispered, "Here's a little lesson for you. See the two men on the right dressed in black? Look closely at their faces; you can see the hate in their eyes. The other four men don't have that look. Those are the two bad boys."

"Yeah, I can see the hate." I remembered seeing that same hateful look when I fought the two al-Qaida men at the church. They have a lot of hate in them for some reason.

The Captain turned and faced the prisoners. "I want to know who killed the old man, Mr. Jackson?"

One of the men spoke up. "Jack, it's me Habib."

I glared at his face. He had a full beard and long hair. I didn't recognize him at first, but I knew that voice. It was Habib. He used to be the General Manager for the golf course here. I used to go to the club house bar every Wednesday. Habib is a little thin guy, standing no more than five and a half feet tall. His hair and beard are jet black.

I walked up to him. "Habib, I thought you left here a long time ago."

"No. I've been here all this time, with my wife and kid. We had no other place to go that was safe."

George asked, "Jack, you know this man?"

"Habib, this is Captain Baldwin. Captain, Habib. He was the GM for this place when it was a golf course."

Habib smiled, showing his yellowish teeth. "It's my great pleasure to meet you, Captain."

"Yeah. Cut the bullshit, which one of you

killed the old man?"

One of the men dressed in black yelled something in Arabic to Habib. "Habib, what did he say?" I asked.

"He said if I tell you anything he'll kill me and my family."

I pulled Habib aside, about ten feet away from the group. "Don't worry, Habib, he's not gonna kill anybody. Tell us, did he do it?"

"Yes, he did it. The two men in black are brothers. They're al-Qaida fighters. The woman in Burqa is their sister. Watch out for her, she's a blood-thirsty bitch."

"Pete, tie the woman in burqa up," Baldwin ordered.

Pete went over to tie her hands. As he approached her she suddenly pulled a large butcher knife out from under her robe. She managed to slash Pete across the face giving him a long bleeding gash on his cheek. Pete promptly bashed the knife-wielding bitch in the face, knocking her to the ground. He ripped off her burqa and tied her up.

Her brothers jumped at Pete, even though their hands were tied behind their backs. Jeff and Pete quickly knocked the two to the ground, using their weapons. The bad guys kept shouting something in Arabic.

George said, "Shut them the hell up."Jeff gagged them while slapping them around.

Pete's gash was bleeding profusely, so Jeff tended to his face.

George, standing next to us asked, "Habib, are you al-Qaida?"

"Shit no! I'm not al-Qaida or ISIS. I'm an American and proud of it. Jack, you know me and my family. We've lived here 25 years."

"Yes, I know you, but I don't know these other people."

George asked, "Who are these three guys?"

"These are my brothers," as he pointed to them. "Only the two men in black are al-Qaida." Habib spit in their direction.

One of the al-Qaida men tried to growl some words through the gag. Pete promptly bashed him in the face, knocking him to the ground again. The other man made a move toward Pete, so Jeff quickly wacked him in the face.

I closely observed Habib's three brothers.

They looked younger. A lot younger because they couldn't grow a full beard. They definitely resembled Habib, because of their height, weight, and shape of their long hooked nose. I recall that he once told me he had three younger brothers. I had no choice but to believe Habib was telling the truth. Why would he lie?

I asked, "Habib, how did you get involved with these al-Qaida guys?"

"They managed to stay here after the Army drove out the main al-Qaida group. They made me hide them. If I didn't, they would kill my whole family. I had no choice."

"Boss, what now?" Pete asked.

"Get the big guy ready." With that comment, Pete and Jeff proceeded to beat the shit out of the bigger man. After a few minutes into the bloody beating, George looked at the man. He was almost knocked out and couldn't put up any type of a struggle. "Ok, that's enough. Drag him over to that bench and hang his head over the back."

I warned Habib, "Don't let your kids see this." He told his wife to cover their eyes.

Jeff and Pete held the man on the wooden bench, forcing his head down so it hung over the back. Captain Baldwin walked up to him and drew out his sword. The man tried to struggle but he was held firm. Baldwin raised the sword over his head and looked around to make sure the man's brother was watching.

Then, in one swift move, he swung the sword with all his might. I heard George grunt as the blade struck. The head fell to the ground with a plop. After wiping the blood off the blade, George sheathed his sword.

Picking the head up by the hair, he stepped over to the other man and held it up in front of his face. "If your kind comes here, this is what you'll get. Habib, does he understand English?"

"Yes, Captain. He fully understands."

Jeff got in his face and rubbed it in. "No head, no heaven, and no virgins."

"I'm letting you go free, to tell your buddies what we did here. Tell them that Captain George Bladwin of the Knights Templar did this. If they come here, they'll get the same treatment. We show no mercy."

Baldwin ordered his men to take him and his sister down the road, over the bridge to I-275 five miles away, and let them go.

"Jack, what should we do with Habib and his family?" Baldwin asked.

I eyeballed Habib and his brothers. He was clearly scared to death, wondering what their fate would be.

I replied, "I've known Habib for many years. He's not dangerous. However, I don't know his brothers."

Habib spoke, "Jack, I can tell you my brothers are just like me. You can trust us. They are not al-Qaida or ISIS. I promise you that. That's the honest truth."

While thinking about the situation, it occurred to me we could use Habib and his family to help improve this area. "Here's what I propose. Habib, you and your family can stay here to live. We're trying to bring law and order to this area and make it safe for normal honest people to live here. Do you wanna help us?"

"Of course, Jack. This is our home. We have no other place to live. What do you want us to do?"

"You and your family will be our eyes and ears here, along with Bill and Ted Cramer. We'll give you a radio and if you see any strangers, let us know right away. Don't take any action. Let us take care of the problem. Captain Baldwin and his men are trained to do that."

"Ok, that sounds great. We'll have your protection. I feel better already."

"That's good, but here's the drawback. If I find out that your brothers are radical Islamists, then you'll lose your head. Does that sound fair?"

Baldwin asked, "Are you sure we can trust them?"

I put my hand on George's shoulder. "I'm ninety-nine percent sure."

Habib commented, "Jack, you can be one hundred percent sure we will be good citizens. You'll see."

"I really hope so, for your sake and your families. We'll be clearing all these buildings over the next few days, so stay inside and don't go roaming around near our men. I don't want you to get killed by mistake. After that, we'll have daily and nightly patrols come around. Also, we're setting up road blocks at each bridge to prevent people from entering."

"You're going to stop everyone from coming here?" Habib asked.

"No, not everyone. Our plan is to allow people in, who pass our interview, or those that have lived here before. So part of your job will be to welcome these people and help them get settled."

"That sounds great to me. You know I'm a friendly guy."

"Yeah. Think of it this way; you're going to be like the Mayor and we're the police. We're also going to give you seeds and plants so you can grow your own food. If you need fishing equipment, then we'll supply it."

Captain Baldwin was getting restless. "Jack, you continue here while my men and I start clearing the buildings again."

"Ok Captain. I think everything is under control here. Thanks for your good work."

"Habib, do you know if any other people live around here?" Baldwin asked.

"Actually, I don't know. There might be some, but I've never seen anyone other than Bill and Ted."

"Jack, what should we do with this body?"Baldwin asked.

"Dump it over the seawall, into the water;

the sharks will eat it."

Everyone watched as Baldwin's men picked up the body, along with the head, and took it away. There was a large wet spot of blood on the ground as a reminder of what just happened.

Habib asked, "Do we get to keep our weapons?"

I replied, "Yes. Bill and Ted still have theirs. Only use them for self-defense. Let's go inside and see what you have." Following Habib and his family into the club house I noticed the room smelled like pot. "Who's been smoking pot?"

"The al-Qaida guys. We never touch the stuff. You know I don't drink either." Habib went over to a corner, pulled a drawer open, and handed me a two pound bag.

I handed it to Bill. "Here, do you guys smoke?"

"A little, thanks," Bill replied with a smile.

"Habib, where are the guns?" I followed him into the next room. Sitting on the floor were eight AK47's, and several hand grenades. There was a box of ammo on the floor with a dozen mags.

I asked Habib, "Why didn't these guys put

up a fight? You got plenty of weapons here."

"To tell you the truth, when they saw your Hummers, with machine guns, they knew you had them out-gunned. But they didn't fight because of their sister and her kid."

"Kid? Is one of these kids her child?"

Habib called the name Abdul. A little boy walked over to us. He was about five years old. "This is her child. I promised her if they were killed or captured I would look after him. I'm sorry I didn't tell you sooner, but I didn't think it was important. He's only a little kid."

"What's his name?"

"Abdul Adi."

I looked at the kid and his eyes showed the same evil look that the others did. "The boy should have went with his mother," I said.

"She's out on the road with no guns and no place to sleep. Great harm might come to the boy."

"Yeah, I guess you're right. I am counting on you to watch him closely and teach him we're his friends. He just saw his uncle's head cut off and his mother beat up."

Habib said, "Jack, don't move. Abdul, put down the gun. Put the gun down now!"

I turned to see little Abdul, fifteen feet away, holding an AK. I froze not knowing what to do. If he was a man, I would have shot him right off the bat. He was pointing the weapon at me when he said, "Infidel ... Allahua Akbar," and tried to pull the trigger.

The kid was too weak to pull the trigger or the safety was on. The AK has a eight pound trigger pull. Habib quickly grabbed the gun out of Abdul's hands and loudly scolded him in Arabic. We were very lucky no one was hurt. Habib looked at the gun and smiled. "The safety was on."

"See Habib, that's what I'm talking about. This kid is trouble."

"I know, I know, I'm very sorry, Jack. His uncle beat him, making him learn the holy books. He was teaching him to hate all none-believers."

It reminded me a little of Adam and the beatings he was given learning the Bible. I couldn't hold it against the kid but I knew he was going to be trouble for sure.

"Well, you got your hands full with him. You're gonna have to teach him not all people are bad. I suggest you keep those guns away from the children or you might get shot. Lock them up in the locker room."

"Ok, I'll do that. Again, I'm very sorry. Abdul, say you're sorry to Mr. Gunn."

Abdul was crying as he said, "Me sorry, Mr. Gunn."

I patted his head. "Don't ever do that again, Abdul. You understand?" He nodded his head and ran over to Habib's wife. "Let's make a supply list of what you might need right now. Bill, you got any ideas?"

Bill and Ted were standing there in shock that the kid tried to kill me. Ted said, "Man, the kid just tried to kill you."

"Yeah, he didn't know what he was doing. Now, let's make a supply list. What items do you need to become self-sufficient here? First of all, I'm bringing everyone some razor blades to shave off those beards."

Ted commented, "Yeah, we don't need these beards anymore, thank God."

Habib said, "We could make a few gardens if we had seeds or some plants."

I said, "Yeah, you'll need some garden tools, also." Habib nodded in agreement.

Bill commented, "Ted and I are pretty good at fishing. We have some gear but could use a net to catch bait fish."

"Actually, I need some fishing gear, just a couple of rods and reels," Habib advised.

I said, "Ok. This is a good start. I'll bring the stuff here tomorrow along with a couple of radios. Anyone got any questions?" No one replied. "Alright then, I'll see you sometime tomorrow."

We shook hands and as I walked out the door I yelled, "Habib, don't forget to lock up those guns!"

Baldwin and his men were busy clearing buildings. It was getting late so I decided to walk the mile and a half home because Mike had my truck. I needed the exercise anyway. I broke into a slow jog. It felt good running; I love to run because it makes me feel alive. I noticed the wind was blowing from the north. Glancing at the bended palm tree leaves, I surmised the wind was blowing about 20 mph. That meant a cold front was coming.

After about half a mile, I stopped to watch a

fish hawk scoop its prey out of the water, on the wing. It was a beautiful sight to see. It was peaceful, so I sat there for half an hour.

The fish hawk is called an Osprey. They resemble Bald Eagles, but smaller. The Bald Eagle hunts fish in the same manner. I envy their eye sight and skill at hunting. It's really very amazing how they pluck a tiny fish out of the water while flying.

They dive from high in the air, zooming down, and at the last minute they flair out their wings to reduce the speed. Gliding over the water they extend their talons just under the surface by an inch or so and whala there's a fish. The fish hawk pulls up, flapping its wings to gain altitude, while holding the wiggling prey. They always land in the same spot to devour their catch, which is high atop a tree or pole. The hawk holds the prey tight until it stops moving. It lets out a loud screech, and then using its sharp beak, it rips the fish open.

Continuing home, I stopped to chat with Chris who was on guard duty on bridge. Chris asked, "How's it going over there?"

"It's going good. The Templars are

incredible. I'm sure glad they're on our side," I said. I proceeded to tell Chris how Baldwin cut off the guy's head.

"Wow, that's pretty intense. Why didn't Baldwin just shoot him?"

"He claims it scares the shit out them to lose their head. No head, then no virgins in heaven."

Chris laughed a little. "When you think about that, it makes a lot of sense."

"I don't know. Maybe so, but I think they could get pissed off and come back."

"Jack, you worry too much."

"It's my job to worry. I gotta go, how about giving me a ride to the Green Room."

Sure enough, sitting in the Green Room was Mike and Lisa. "Hey Jack, what's up? How's the clearing going?" Mike was a little drunk and so was Lisa.

"I thought you were coming back to pick me up. You missed a lot of action. What happened to the old lady?"

"Sorry to say, she didn't make it. That's why we're here having a drink. We're having a celebration of life, so to speak. Tomorrow I'm gonna get her husband and bury them together at sea."

I poured a drink, took a sip, and lit up a smoke. "You missed Baldwin in action. We found two al-Qaida fighters and he cut one's head off."

"No shit. That's over doing it a bit, isn't it?"

"He has his reasons." I slapped Mike on the back. "I'm going home for dinner. I'll see you tomorrow."

I drove my Humvee home and arrived just in time for dinner at 6 pm. My family was just sitting down as I walked in the back door. Adolf greeted me with a wagging tail. It was good to be home. I put my M4 in the safe. I usually wear my Glock at all times, but tonight I took it off.

After dinner, Adam asked me, "You wanna look at the map some more?" I could tell he was expecting me to say yes.

"Sure," I replied, "You go on up and I'll be there in a few minutes."

I told the adult members of my family what happened today. They all knew Habib, and were surprised that he was living in the old clubhouse. Then I told them about the two al-Qaida fighters we found.

Tommy commented, "Damn, they were living in our backyard so to speak." What did you do with those guys? Kill them?"

"Baldwin killed one and let the woman and the other one go free." I didn't tell them that Baldwin cut off one of their heads.

My son-in-law, Jim Bo, said, "What do you mean, let them go?"

"He had his men take them to I-275 and let them go. I think, I don't know for sure. Maybe they did kill them on the side of the road." Then it occurred to me that maybe they really did kill them.

Hemmi asked, "How long before that area is safe?"

"Honey, I don't know for sure, maybe a couple of weeks. Why?"

"Most of us women have been stuck on this island for a year or more. It would be nice to meet some new people, just to get off of this island."

"Yeah, you're right as always. I'll tell you what, tomorrow I have to take some supplies to Habib and the others. Why don't you and Amy come along and help out for a couple of hours. You could meet Habib's wife."

Hemmi smiled. "Ok, that sounds great. What time do we leave?"

"I was thinking sometime around noon. We'll take them some food as a gift."

"I'll make a special treat for them."

"Ok, that sounds good. I'm going upstairs to talk with Adam for a while."

Arriving at Adams room, I knocked on the door. "It's me."

"Grandpa, come in," Adam shouted.

Adam had the U.S. map spread out on the bed. "Did you find anything new?" I asked.

"Well, not really, but I was thinking. All these guys like De Soto, Ponce de Leon, Cortez, and so forth, didn't come to Florida by mistake. They had some kind of map or information. They were looking for the treasure. I have no doubt about it.

"De Soto came to the west coast of Florida first. Both he and Cortez sailed through the dangerous Florida Keys. Cortez kept sailing west and found Mexico in 1518. It wasn't until 1539 that Hernando de Soto landed in Tampa Bay. Why did he come here of all places?"

Adam paused and I said, "I don't know, but go ahead, you're making a lot of sense."

"Well, I don't know either, but if you follow his trail, he traveled north by land through Florida and then west to the Mississippi River. He discovered the Mississippi."

While peering at the map I commented, "I think you're right. He traveled around the southern end of Florida and headed north, just like the clues on the sword state."

"Yes, and furthermore, the great river that flows out of the north has to be the Mississippi."

"I think you're on to something. Then where did he go?"

Adam touched my shoulder. "He died there from battle wounds and a fever in 1542. The expedition ended when he died."

Shaking Adam's hand, I said, "Great job. I think you're exactly right. The great river that flows from the north is the Mississippi. Now we just have to find what other large river flows into the Mississippi from the west."

"Yes. That's what I'm looking for now. If

we can find that then it could be our starting point. Do you think they used a compass of some kind?"

"Yeah. It's a known fact that the Vikings used a rough magnetic compass, so I'm sure the Templars had one. The sword says the summer solstice sun will light the way. So we got some time before that happens," I told Adam.

"When is that exactly?"

"It varies, but it's sometime in mid-June. We can find the exact date later."

"Gee whiz, that's nine months away, Grandpa."

"Yep, but it might take us a couple of months to find the spot. The problem is, if we don't find the right location when the solstice happens, we'll have to wait another year," I advised Adam.

"Wow, I never thought of that. This isn't so easy, is it?"

I chuckled a little. "No, it's not easy. We have to be in the right location at the right time or we'll never find the treasure. Adam, I'm gonna hit the hay now. Don't stay up too late."

Adam hugged me and replied, "Thanks Grandpa. This is really fun working with you to find

134

the treasure location. Good night."

"Yep, it's fun. You did a good job." I rubbed the top of his head messing up his hair. "Good night."

I went downstairs for a smoke and poured a double shot. Tommy and Adolf were sitting on the patio. It seemed that everyone else was in bed or getting ready for bed. Tommy asked me, "Ok, tell me what really happened with Baldwin today?"

"I didn't wanna say anything in front of the women, but he cut the head off of one al-Qaida fighter. He really did let the other two go free so they would tell their friends. Baldwin's theory is they're scared to get their heads cut off, so they won't come around here anymore."

"I hope he's right. Hey, what are you and Adam working on?"

"We're trying to find the treasure location."

"Why? Are you going treasure hunting?" Tommy asked.

"At first, I didn't want anything to do with it. Now I think it could be a once in a lifetime adventure. It would really be something to find the Ark."

"If you found it, what would you do with it?"

"That's a good question. I haven't thought about that."

Tommy walked into the kitchen and poured us both another drink. Coming back he asked, "Do you have any idea where it is?"

"Yeah, it's out west." I took a sip of booze. "It's pretty far away."

"Well you've been out west a lot. It's a big place. You could hide a treasure anywhere. Is that all you know, it's out west?"

"I'm not a hundred percent sure of the exact location, but I know the general location. I haven't told Adam yet because I want him to find it."

"Ok, tell me the general location." Tommy asked.

"I don't wanna say where right now. When I'm positive, I'll tell you."

"What are you gonna do make an expedition and go search for it?"

Yeah, that's what I'm thinking of doing. I wanna be like Indiana Jones and look for lost artifacts." I chuckled a little.

Tommy glanced at me. "Dad, you have no idea what's out west. It's probably more dangerous than here. You better think this over."

"I have thought it over. I'll need the Templars, the four Humvees, four big pick-up trucks, a bunch of guns, and an airplane."

"What's the plane for?"

I put my smoke out and took a sip of whiskey. "I was thinking of using it for scouting. Rick and Jim Bo can fly small planes. If one of their planes are still in working condition, I'll use them to scout the road ahead."

"When do you plan on doing this?"

"According to the sword, the summer solstice, which is in June, will light the way to the treasure. We'll need to leave Tocabaga in April."

"Doing that means you're pulling a lot of fire power away from Tocabaga."

"I won't go if the Rangers aren't back by then. Hey, I'm gonna hit the sack. Good night."

Tommy replied, "I don't think this expedition is a good idea because it's too dangerous. That's all I got to say about it. Goodnight." I could tell by Tom's tone of voice, he was upset with me.

Climbing into bed, I found my wife was already asleep. My mind was racing, thinking about the treasure. I had gold fever. Only it wasn't for gold. It was for something far more important. April will be here in seven months. I still had to narrow down the area where the treasure might be located. I couldn't stop thinking about it.

Not being able to sleep, I got out of bed and went down to the computer. I searched the ACWWW, which is the same as the internet but it's controlled by the Army. ACWWW stands for Army Command World Wide Web. Captain Sessions provided me a password a while back. This was the first time for me to use it.

I typed in the search box, 'Old Army Trails.' I guessed that someone must have mapped the old trails. I knew they had to follow the trails established by the American Indians hundreds of years ago. After searching through several hundred maps, I finally found one that showed a trail headed in a westerly direction.

Satisfied with my findings, I went to bed

thinking I had almost solved the problem. All I had to do now was determine what the land marks were.

If you have any ideas where the treasure is located, let me know.

Email me at tocabaga.jack@gmail.com. I WILL REPLY.

That's all for now.

GOD BLESS AMERICA, LAND OF THE FREE, and HOME OF THE BRAVE!

Jack Gunn, a.k.a. Tocabaga Jack

THOMAS H. WARD

DRAMATIS PERSONAE
TOCABAGA

Adam de Molay – A future Knights Templar leader. Sent to Jack, by God.

Abdul Adi – A five old kid who tried to kill Jack.

Albert Madison – Navy Vet. who comes to Tocabaga with his wife and two   kids.

Army Mike – Retired Army combat vet, we just call him Mike.

Barry – A quisling killed by the Gunn family.

Billy – Kid found living on the street with his sister Rosie and brother Peter.

Bill and Ted Cramer – Preppers living in the ruins near Tocabaga.

Brogan – A Tocabaga security guard who went MIA.

Bok Lam – A Chinese man and close friend of Jack's since high school.

Buck – Motorcycle gang leader killed by Maggie.

Chase – A quisling.

Colonel Turner – Commanding Officer of the Army Rangers based at Fort Desoto.

Colonel Park - aka Captain Kim a South Korean spy working for China.

Corporal Phillips – In charge of the communications office at Fort Desoto.

Captain George Baldwin – A Knights Templar commander.

Captain Sessions – Combat officer, commands and controls combat operations in the field.

Captain Riley – Female tank commander, girl friend of Captain Sessions.

Captain Zhu Lei – A commie killed by Tommy.

Chris – Tocabaga security guard and close friend of Jack.

Christian de Molay – Adam de Molay's uncle. A self proclaimed Grand Master.

Daniel Gibbs – Bad guy from a convoy on Interstate 75.

Dew – A quisling killed by the Gunn family.

Dirty Dan – Leader of the 22nd Avenue gang.

Dr. Carl Urban – The inventor of the RCCD Units and friend of Jack's.

Dr. Carl Urban, Jr. – Son of Dr. Urban.

Dr. Alvin Sinclair – Robot inventor and Commie killed by Jack.

Ellen – A lonely woman.

Emma de Molay – The sister of Adam found on Interstate 75.

Freddy Hammon – A gang member.

First Lt. Fisher – TALOS Warrior, Platoon commander.

Farmer John – An old farmer saved by Jack, now living on Tocabaga.

Guy Allen or GA – Suspected spy living on Tocabaga was killed by Jack.

General Chen – A Red Chinese Army General in charge of the Florida   invasion force.

General Harper – Commander of the Rangers located at SOCOM.

George Taylor – A nice kid who was bullied in school by Nick.

Grandpa Jack – Jack de Moley the Knights Templar Grand Master.

Hemmi – Wife of Jack Gunn.

Habib – General Manger of the old club house.

Jace – A Tocabaga citizen.

Joe – RCCD tech. Supervisor; a tough guy killed by Jack.

Little Johnny – Adopted grandson of Jack's.

Johnny the Fisherman – A quisling killed by security.

Jill – A warrior killed by Feds.

Jim Bo – Husband to Amy and son-in-law of Jack.

Jimmy Smith – A bully from years ago.

Ken – US Deputy Marshal who went missing.

Leroy – The man who killed Jack's little brother Mike.

Lee – A Chinese invisible.

Malcolm – A dissatisfied citizen of Tocabaga.

Mike – Jack Gunn's little brother killed by a doper.

Maggie – Wife of Robbie, who is in charge of the

farming.

Mr. Johnson or Famer John – Old time Farmer.

Mr. Horn – Pig farmer and dirt bag who wanted to kidnap Maggie for   breeding.

Nick – A bully from Junior High School.

Reed Gurra – A gang member.

Peter – Little nine year old brother to Rosie.

Rosie – A fifteen year old girl Jack found living on the street.

Robbie – Best friend of Jack Gunn, killed by the FPF on April 27, 2025.

Ron – Brother of Jack Gunn Retired Navy vet. Part of Tocabaga security.

Rick – President of Tocabaga Association, security team member.

Sam Smith – Leader of a convoy of bad dangerous people.

Sally – A warrior killed by Feds.

Scotty – A quisling killed by security.

Sergeant Hammer – Army Ranger.

Sergeant First Class Dale – killed in action.

Sergeant Major Willis – Ranger squad leader and security guard for Jack.

Sergeant Cain – the Drone Master.

Sergeant Smith - Army Ranger assigned as security guard for Jack.

Stan – Deputy Marshal.

Sue – Wife of Albert Madison.

Tommy Gunn – Son of Jack Gunn and a retired Marine Scout Sniper.

Tony – Bar keeper and sharp-shooter for Tocabaga security.

Trini – Amazon Warrior who killed Troy.

Troy – A quisling killed by security.

Victor Elway – An old farmer from Ellenton now living on Tocabaga with his   friend Farmer John.

Zack – A quisling killed by the Gunn family.

Read the rest of

The Tocabaga Chronicles

By Thomas H. Ward

TOCABAGA 1: Revised Edition

TOCABAGA 2: Theoterrorism

TOCABAGA 3: Warm Blood – Cold Steel

TOCABAGA 4: Talos Warriors

TOCABAGA 5: The Quislings & Adroktones

TOCABAGA 6: The Dimachaerus Clan - Missing In Action

TOCABAGA 7: Pàn Guó Zuì - HIGH TREASON

TOCABAGA 8: The Invisibles

TOCABAGA 9: THE CRIMSON CROSS

To Contact the author:

Visit his website: www.ThomasHWardBooks.com

Or by email: tocabaga.jack@gmail.com

THOMAS H. WARD

www.ingramcontent.com/pod-product-compliance
Lightning Source LLC
Chambersburg PA
CBHW071947170626
46813CB00005B/1862